Cycle

✠

The light is still
At the still point of the turning world.

Burnt Norton
T.S. ELIOT

Cycle

JAY AMBERG

Whale Song previously published in 2011 by Amika Press.

Cycle

© Copyright 2012, Jay Amberg & Amika Press

First Edition   ISBN 13: 978-1-937484-00-2

AMIKA PRESS

466 Central Ave STE 6   Northfield IL 60093   847 869 8084
info@amikapress.com   Available for purchase on amikapress.com
Twenty percent of all proceeds will be donated to The Nature Conservancy.
Edited by John Manos.
Designed by Sarah Koz in Adobe InDesign. Body set in 11/16.5 Fleischman BT Pro, designed by J.M. Fleischman in 1730, digitized by Charles Gibbons in 2002. Titles set in Koch Antiqua, designed by Rudolph Koch in 1922, digitzed by Linotype in 2007. Ornaments set in P22 Koch Signs, designed by Rudolph Koch in 1930, digitzed by Denis Kegler in 1997. Thanks to Nathan Matteson.

Thanks to John Manos
for his insightful reading
and to Sarah Koz
for her superb designs

Here the impossible union
Of spheres of existence is actual

The Dry Salvages
T.S. ELIOT

Redwood Ring

Come. Stand among us for a moment on this flat above the rolling river. Be wholly here. Root for a time. You are alone—good. We are a ring, never alone, each identical and each different, one life entwined at root and crown. We are the descendents of deep time, of earth, air, water, and light.

The soil beneath us is dark, rich, and deep. Drops of mist fall from our canopy three hundred feet through silver air to the brown duff, the fallen needles and decaying plants covering the ground. Light dances on the river, but here within our ring it barely dapples the duff. Bright gnats swirl through still air.

A community thrives within our ring. Our life is a gift beyond reason and measure. Beyond measure and reason, our life makes sense. But only if you stand among us will you understand us, this place, this time in which we live. Get to know us, our world, before we are gone, before it is gone.

ᛦ

We are a redwood ring. We have stood on this alluvial flat for 823 years—not ancient by earth's time, but far older than almost all other living organisms. A few of our close relatives are well over 1500 years old.

To the west, the river, now brown with silt, bends toward the ocean. The river's bank rises sharply for thirty-seven feet, protecting us, most often, from floods. The valley's half-mile-high slopes also protect us, at least sometimes, from the most severe storms. Time shears both the banks and slopes. Our grove, interspersed with fir and pine and broadleaf trees, now covers twenty thousand acres.

The tallest of us in the ring is 319 feet, the shortest, our albino, only forty-two. Nearby redwoods rise above 350 feet, but none of us will likely reach that height. The thickest of us is thirty-nine feet in circumference. Broad, certainly, but nowhere near the girth of some of the neighboring giants. Originally thirteen of us encircled our parent, but three of us have been windthrown, two in the terrific storm 154 years ago, and one just last year. So, though we remain a ring, we are no longer a circle.

We do not have individual brains, but we are as a ring mindful. In any grove, it is always every tree for itself, of course, but here that truism is not exactly true. We understand life—just as this forest does, just as the earth itself does. We are cognizant of diurnal rhythms and solar rotations. We stand; we do not stand for something else.

We respond to the world each moment. Every moment is integral within the cycles, and every moment is present for us. We are rooted in earth, nourished by air and water, and growing toward light. We need all four, but light, ultimately, gives us—and everything else—life.

Who exactly are we? Well, obviously, we are trees, the largest of all plants. As trees, we have roots, trunks, branches, leaves, and seeds. We grow fast, spiraling into the sky toward light, and continue to grow as long as we live.

Though we are the tallest of all earth's organisms and our groves have the greatest terrestrial biomass on the planet, our roots do not run deep. We have no taproots that bore straight down. Rather, our roots spread shallowly, penetrating only ten feet or so but extending out a hundred. Our roots interlock, providing much more mutual stability than any one of us would have alone.

Our evergreen leaves are shaped like needles. Toward our conical crowns, our needles grow smaller and more tightly together. Our cones are tiny, only the size of olives, but each of us may still spew more than a million seeds a year.

At our core is heartwood, our oldest wood, which adds strength and resilience. Sapwood surrounds our heartwood. Sap, water and minerals, flows from the soil through our roots and trunk to our branches and needles. Beyond our sapwood is our cambium, which produces new wood. It grows swiftly but changes our appearance by only the width of one ring each year—sometimes less than an inch and sometimes more, depending on the cycle's mood.

Our inner bark sends sugars from our needles to every other part of our bodies, right down to our root tips. Our outer bark is thick, fibrous, red, and furrowed with ridges. The color comes from our tannin, a chemical that resists fungi, fire, and flood. Our bark also protects us from insects and pretty much everything else. We live so long because we really have no natural enemies.

We were born of fire—that most energetic of earth's light. Fires occur naturally here, but not often—and never spontaneously. Oxygen unites with other substances all the time, but a fire starts only when that union is swift. To exist, fire needs fuel and oxygen and enough heat to ignite. Our grove provides abundant oxygen and plenty of fuel, especially in the late summer when the duff is less damp, but seldom is there enough heat for ignition. Here, lightning usually provides that necessary spark, though occasionally flames invade from other regions, climbing ridge after ridge until they reach us.

Most fires crawl along the ground, consuming duff and ferns, seedlings and saplings and thin-barked trees. The flames, flickering only a foot or two in the air, check disease and kill hosts of bacteria and fungi. Our bark, eight to ten inches thick, insulates us. We also lack resin and pitch, which attract flame, and so, though we are often scarred, we seldom succumb. New growth has masked most, but not all, of our scars. Seven of us still bear scars, and the easternmost of us has a twenty-foot scar deep enough into the heartwood for a bear to sleep in it.

The rare wildfire leaps from tree to tree, gulping oxygen and swallowing whole branches—feeding far more like an animal than a plant. Its temperature soars, and its light bounds. Living on this flat, we have been lucky enough to escape the two 1000-degree fires in our life. The river thwarted the spread of the first, and the second, just two hundred years ago, leapt past us along the far ridge.

Our parent, deeply scarred by earlier conflagrations, was enveloped by a wildfire. The flames climbed the trunk and inhaled the crown. Only the charred stump, the burl just beneath the ground, and the roots remained. We began life together in our parent's burl, a knobby clump of dormant buds buried in the ash. The fire woke us, and we sprang in a circle around the scorched remains, each of us genetically identical to our parent. Our roots interlaced with our parent's and each other's. We sprouted through the rich, nutritious ash into the sunlight created when the fire razed the canopy—and became, in a deep sense, our own parent.

Though our genes are all the same, our responses to the world are, through the fullness of time, distinct. In every moment, each of us reacts to light and water, sun and storms, wind and flood, drought and fire—and the earth itself. We share the same predispositions but live at the whim of nature. Each of us has a different height and girth. We all have 823 rings, but none of our rings is identical. Each of us has a crown that shapes our shared canopy. From a common root system, we grow diverse boles, burls, and branches. Each of us, in unison, is unique, and all are one.

So, genetics drives us—but in divergent ways. We respond to each other's lives and to the lives of others, the infinitesimal and the immense, the fungi and the fir in our midst. Only two of us rise purely vertically; the others, always seeking light, lean from five to fifteen degrees. Ten of us have multiple trunks, iterations of ourselves, trees growing out of trees. One splits just above the duff, and another has grown, at thirty feet, a horizontal buttress that supports a forty-seven-inch-thick secondary bole. Our albino, of course, produces only ivory-white needles that lack chlorophyll.

We stem from the oldest living woody plants on earth. Sixty million years ago, our ancestors covered much of this continent, much of this hemisphere. But spreading ice and uplifting mountains cut our population to a small fraction and drove us northwest toward the coast. Though we depend on fog, salt spray harms us—so we thrive just inland. The temperate climate and winter rains suit us. Here our forest became stable.

Stability doesn't, however, suggest stagnation. Our ring and this grove always grow, always change. The grove's canopy is deep and multilayered. Most nearby trees are more than two hundred years old, but each stand adds two or three trees per century. And each stand loses about the same number to wind and fire and flood. Around us, among the woody debris, fallen trunks lie in various stages of decay—an ongoing reformation of matter. The grove, quite simply, exists within a stable cycle of birth, growth, death, decay, and birth again, all the while recycling the same chemicals. And within this cycle, myriad organisms, including us, wheel through our lives.

Time slows in this grove, but it never stops. Though time rings, we ourselves always live in the present. We are scarred by wind and fire, but we barely age physiologically. Ephemera appear and disappear, both individuals and species. We provide a home, a world even, for generations upon generations—newts and slugs, voles and chickarees, spotted owls and marbled murrelets. They creep or scramble or flap about, but we are. The seasons turn, our ring alters, and our rings accumulate.

Our roots, enmeshed with our parent's and our older forebears', have been alive for five thousand years. Through our shared roots and genes, the flow of light each day, and the coursing of the seasons, experience accrues. We travel through time, but we remain present. Our time, each moment and the flowing spiral itself, abides.

We feel energy all about us, within and without. The earth harbors it, the river flows with it, the air trembles with it, the wind carries it, and fire bursts with it. Life teems with it. It shifts, rests, converts, lies dormant, and erupts. Whatever its current form, all energy emanates from the sun; all of it is, or once was, solar energy.

Energy converts—form to form. Lightning strikes a spruce far up the slope. Fire consumes the tree, heat and light licking the sky. Wind whips the flames, and before rain douses the fire, five acres smolder and char. The snag topples, knocking down another fire-scarred tree. Storms saturate the ground, and the topsoil slides to the river, taking the fallen boles with it. Dammed water pools, then sluices, cutting a new course. And energy pulses through all of it in every moment.

Our energy is more subtle than that of storm, fire, landslide, and flood, but it's still pervasive. It permeates the entwining of our roots, the expansion of our cambium, the rise of our sap, the spiral of our trunk, the turn toward sun of our twigs and needles, and our transformation of light.

ᚹ

We who are green turn light into food. The sun, our star, vibrates with energy, its pulse repeating about every two minutes. It radiates electromagnetic energy, at once both particle and wave, at a fantastic, but finite, speed. We feel the constant vibrations and receive the radiation across space and time. The earth's atmosphere blocks much of the radiation but not all of the heat and light. The sun's energy flows through us, alters, and passes on to all living creatures.

The sun is, of course, the source of the earth's energy past, present, and future, but we use light *directly*. Our sapwood carries water from our roots to our needles, and our needles pull carbon dioxide from the air. Sunshine activates the chlorophyll in our chloroplasts, which then splits the water into hydrogen and oxygen.

The hydrogen and light energy break down the carbon dioxide. All of these combine into sugar. The by-product, oxygen, flows from our needles, helping to form the earth's atmosphere and to enable animals to breathe. And our inner bark transfers the sugar from our needles to our other parts. This cycle binds earth and light and water and air, plants and animals, star and planet. The transformation engenders and sustains our life—all of our lives.

YY

Night still matters. Starlight doesn't bathe us—in fact, it barely touches us. The aurora flicks us with energy, but only slightly. The moon's cycle is not ours. Stars turn with the seasons, but their song is distant. And yet, dark makes all the difference.

As day fades to evening, our transformation of light slows and stops. We no longer cast off oxygen. But our respiration, the opposite and the complement of the transformation, continues at a steady rate. Our rate of respiration changes considerably with the seasons but not so much with the time of day. In the dark, we go on utilizing the energy we have created. We continue to use nutrients and slough carbon dioxide. We grow.

Indeed, we grow more in the dark than in light. Our transformation of light consumes us in the moments in which it is occurring. At night, our cambium can more readily create us. So, the light of day and its transformation are the basis of life, but night, darkness, is necessary as well. Each reciprocates the other, and both are parts of the whole, the fullness of the daily cycle.

YY

Our lives flow through water. Without it, neither we nor any other organism can live. Our transformation of light wouldn't occur. We are not, though, merely dependent on water: we are water. Water composes far more than half of us, as it does most beings.

Water falls though air, of course (most often here as rain, though sometimes as snow), but our relationship with fog is most intense. Without fog here, drought would kill us. Summer ocean currents and prevailing winds push coastal fog inland. The fog reduces drought-stress by raising humidity and lowering evaporation, but something more happens here with us. As fog drifts over the ridge and settles, we, the tallest organisms around, snatch it. The smaller, tighter needles in our canopy are especially good at snaring moisture. Our downward hanging branches funnel the moisture, and water itself, being always cohesive, forms drops. Fogdrip has sustained us and all our understory's plants in even the driest seasons. Some years, it produces more than a third of the water we consume.

Water vaporizes, vanishing into air, and re-forms. And, whenever it gathers, it runs. Whether in a deluge flushing our ring or in a river cutting a new channel, it always finds its way. Still, the flow of water from our roots to our needles three hundred feet above pushes the edge of possibility. We lift sap through long hollow cells—against gravity—every moment of every day of our lives. As each molecule of water evaporates from our needles, we pull a replacement molecule through our hydraulic system.

Water sticks to itself, to us, to everything. By using its natural adhesiveness, we can raise water to improbable heights—thereby forming a perfect loop of air, soil, and wood that lifts water to the light that creates the world's food. We can regulate the flow by opening and closing the pores in our needles. We can even, when necessary, reverse the flow, take water in through our needles—in essence, drink it.

The only thing we can't do is fix the system when it breaks. If any part of us, particularly near the crown, is damaged, air bubbles can form in our transport cells, and the flow stops—forever.

The music of this world plays all about us in each moment. We feel its vibrations every second of every day of every year of our life. Each moment's notes, each day's rhythms, and each season's varying harmonies touch us to our heartwood. Since we were shoots, we have performed our small parts in the world's continuous symphony.

The air vibrates always, sometimes with the sweet tempo of a breeze, sometimes with storms' crescendos. In turn, air riffles and whisks; our branches thrum, and our needles jingle. Floods pound through our flat, but far more often the river rings on rock as it passes. During droughts, it trills. Rain drums on our canopy, and fogdrip taps the soil above our roots. The hum of our rising sap, its blending with chlorophyll, and the slow respiration in our needles produce a chord both subtle and sublime. Banana slugs slithering through duff, chipmunks skittering along toppled boles, butterflies wafting in and out of light, and salamanders scrambling across ferns in our canopy—all contribute to the chorus. Even the continental plates deep below us intermittently clash, adding their deep tones to the symphony.

The deepest melody, though, is the sun's, which flows to and through us as both discrete notes and concerted tune. Beyond the sun's song is the distant, faint, and contrapuntal pulsing of the other stars. All of the music plays in time and through time within our ring, across our flat, around the world, and out into the vastness.

ᛘ

In recent years, the last hundred or so, the land beyond the ridges has rumbled with a discordant, unnatural din. Distant intermittent crashes have sent tremors through our flat. Often, a buzzing flows through our soil. A constant whirring, too, especially in daylight. None of it echoes the music that has always flowed through each of our days. These dissonant reverberations are new, not altogether comprehensible, and nothing even like the occasional quaking of the continental plates. No, the crashes resemble most windthrown falls during storms, only they have inevitably followed shrill shrieking and have occurred far more frequently—thousands a year rather than a few every century. And, until the last few years, the cacophony has tramped steadily toward us.

For the most part, the shuddering has stopped now, but the whirring continues unabated. In that time of rumbling, though, the forest upstream fell out of balance. The river floods more frequently, and the floods are more severe. The water has all gone brown. More detritus, especially stumps and roots, tangle at times along the bank. Lifeless, they neither give nor take much energy. One massive stump still hangs along the bend below us, its roots shriveling.

ᛃ

We have become a cathedral. Our crowns, like our roots, interweave. Our lower branches, no longer able to find light, have fallen away. Only a few below 180 feet survive. And so our understory is now vaulted, our canopy a dome—another world we compose even as our floor decomposes.

Light undiluted pours into our canopy and suffuses among our needles. The energy of our transformation erupts into sky. Our needles proliferate; our trunks reiterate. Branches buttress, fuse with each other and our trunks, and thrust upward, stabilizing the canopy. Indeed, a new forest thrives, a profusion of life bursting toward light.

Debris accumulates in the crotches among the trunks and branches; organic matter mats, deepens, and forms into rich, thick layers of soil. A whole world grows in the axil of each branch. Moss, lichens, fungi, ferns, shrubs, and even other species of trees—all flourish in our canopy. An eleven-foot hemlock sprouts 280 feet above the ground. Even we send aerial roots into this mass of life.

Marbled murrelets nest in our canopy, as do bats, flying squirrels, and spotted owls. So do a host of terrestrials—slugs, newts, earthworms, millipedes, beetles, even mollusks. Wandering salamanders breed, bring up their young, and die in the damp humus among the fronds. And all of this happens almost three hundred feet above the ground.

ᚥ

Life is life. We are all carbon-based forms. We are all part of this intricate web here on this alluvial flat, in this valley, on this continent, in this biosphere that keeps our planet, our home, alive. We all have the same DNA in different orders of pairs; we are generated and ourselves generate. We are influenced by and respond to our environment. We grow, consume nutrients, give off waste, rest, have sex, and die. All of life does.

On some level, distinctions matter. We plants produce our own food, and animals do not. In fact, animals are, to be perfectly blunt, superfluous. We move by growing; we do not need to move around to survive. And even among plants, we in this ring are distinct. We differ significantly from the fir, more so from the hemlock. Our habitats overlap, and in some ways we compete. But we never try to annihilate others. No species could misunderstand the nature of life's web that badly.

Redwoods dominate this grove. We are better suited to this place in this moment. But as climate changes—as it surely is at present—that may no longer be true. The ephemera may survive better than we do. The creatures in our understory, not just the fir and the hemlock, but many of the smaller plants and animals, will have a better chance. Over time, species come and go. After all, dinosaurs roamed among our ancestors. Though we may perish, life will survive.

Any distinctions, therefore, are, on a deeper level, specious. We are all life. Lichens, for example, abound in our grove. They cling to rock and our bark, rise from the ground, and hang from our branches. Each is a fungus wrapped around an alga in a stunning symbiosis—a single organism. And then there is this: our chlorophyll exists only within our chloroplasts. We don't, strictly, transform light; our chloroplasts do. Perhaps our forebears, deep in time, were like lichens. Indeed, we may well be mammoth, intricate relics of a primordial symbiosis between plant and animal.

Within us, still deeper distinctions blur. Parts of us are, in a sense, already dead. Our heartwood, for instance, that helps keep us strong and flexible isn't really living. But life doesn't, finally, reduce. That which lives and that which doesn't are the same matter, yet *we* are alive.

All life is woven together here on this earth. Others depend on us certainly, but we depend on them as well. We can only exist within the community of life. Even those which seem to do us harm—fungi, for instance—can be helpful. Aren't we all earth, air, light, and water for which at some archaic moment something inexplicable occurred, and we began to live?

ᛉ

And what then to make of the fungi that flourish beneath us? They are incapable of producing their own chlorophyll as we and all other plants do. They can't create their own food, their own energy. They feed on decay; they thrive on rot. They cause disease. They blight our needles and kill our twigs. They destroy the vast majority of our seeds. But they don't kill us. We have grown impervious to them.

In fact, we may not be able to live without fungi. The fir in our midst would already be dead. Some pine would be extinct. As the fungi spread in the soil, their tangled mass of threads absorbs dead and dying organic matter. They wrap their threads around our root tips. They trade the nitrogen and phosphorous that we need for our sugar without which they can't survive. They enhance our intake of water and stimulate us to elongate our roots, extend our root systems, and interlace our roots, connecting us ever more strongly.

Most of the small animals that live with us eat the fungi's fruiting bodies, the mushrooms that sprout above ground and the truffles below. These animals then spread the fungi's spores so that when our surviving seeds later germinate the relationship continues as it has for eons. This ancient, complex, symbiotic connection is the norm—not the exception.

In this grove, we redwoods die mostly by toppling. Lightning can snap a crown and leave a snag, an upright trunk devoid of foliage, but that's rare on this flat. Fungi and insects and arboreal diseases don't much affect us. Fire scars may occasionally, like our parent's, burn too deeply. Intermittently, a flood undercuts the bank of a stream, and roots lose purchase. Once in a great while, a bear strips too much of our bark. But windthrow, especially after winter storms when the ground is saturated, is most common. Whatever the cause, the earth shakes in the moment of passing. The crash reverberates through all of us.

After the downfall, the tree goes on living for a time, sending its nutrients, its energy, its life down through its still entwined roots to those who live around it. We in our ring share our lives and deaths, of course, but so do all the redwoods in this grove.

It's difficult to determine the exact moment of death

for, even in death, we remain integrated with life. And the moment of death is largely irrelevant. Our life, quite literally, precedes and succeeds each of us. We sprouted from our stricken parent, not offspring but genetic clones. Our roots—again, quite literally—are ancient.

The two of us felled in that storm 154 years ago still teem with life, hosting about 4000 species of plants and animals. Herbs and shrubs decorate the decaying bark. Chipmunks bustle atop, and voles hunch beneath, feasting on fruiting fungi. Our wood deteriorates so slowly—over hundreds of years—that generations of amphibians live in our hollows. Salamanders favor the moist undersides of fallen logs nearest the river.

Our recently fallen bole still slips energy to us even as the fungi begin their slow, inexorable task of returning nutrients to the soil. Life already burgeons all along its trunk and upturned roots—lichens and sorrel and ferns spreading over fallen needles. Life, then, is life, but death isn't exactly death.

ᚤ

The problem with animals—other than that they miss out on the transformation of light—is that they are so incredibly needy. Especially mammals. They require so much and do so little except scurry their lives away. They need so much food, none of which they themselves create, and require such protection from each other. They're not exactly parasites, but in their predator-prey relationships they always expend and never provide energy. Some are even nocturnal, avoiding light as though it were anything but the main source of life.

Bats, for example, roost in deep cracks in our bark and in our fire scars. They need what we need—temperatures that aren't extreme, a lot of moisture, and access to water. But these, for them, aren't nearly enough. Our height provides both protection and launching pads for their nocturnal forays. Some spend much of their time preying, and some return soon after snatching insects and moths.

Bats are, of course, part of a natural cycle, just as we are part of daily, seasonal, and lifelong cycles. They are predators, but they are also the prey of spotted owls and other birds. It's all part of the complex web that sustains all living beings. But still—a life of rampaging to eat and cowering so as not to be eaten? A life of constant consumption? A life without light?

Time rings in our ring. After the winter solstice, just beyond the coldest, wettest, darkest moments of the year, our male cones shower our female cones with pollen. Soon rainbell and laurel begin to bloom, wrens sing their territorial songs, and maples leaf out. The river crests, sometimes runs in torrents, and occasionally surges over its banks, silting our flat.

By the vernal equinox, hatchlings skitter in the river's pools, and chipmunks scramble along our fallen trunks. Spotted owls nest, our sorrel blooms, and the rain slackens. As our new needles sprout light green, the first breaths of fog reach us. Deer give birth, and we grow again.

Ladyferns line the riverbank at the summer solstice. Fog flows; mist settles, and we drip for days on end. In early morning, the sky is often a cloudland. By afternoon, light bathes our canopy. Jays squabble, and fawns lose their spots. Red starts to mark the poison oak.

Fog dissipates by the autumnal equinox—but doesn't disappear. The river rolls lazily through the warmest days of the year. Ladybugs congregate, deer mate, oaks drop acorns, rain renews, and our old needles fall to duff. Fungi fruits appear; chipmunks vanish. Fish spawn in the pools as migratory birds pass our canopy. Strong storms brew and thrash, dispersing our seeds by the tens of millions. And the year winds down through dark, dank days.

Each of us is, by nature, androgynous. We each bear male and female reproductive organs. Not halved by gender, we're all able to experience the fullness, the completeness, of our species.

During each year's short, dark days only some of our male cones' pollen reaches our female cones immediately, and even then fertilization doesn't usually occur for weeks. Once our sperm and egg combine, a cell of new life forms and then divides and clusters into a seedling. Each seedling has an embryonic root, shoot tip, and needle leaves. Surrounded by stored food, the seed develops in six months and then slows almost to a stop.

Through the warm, less wet days, our female cones wait for strong autumnal winds. Though our cones shed seeds for months, most seeds fly during these first severe storms. Each of us spreads more than a million seeds a year, but few of them survive. Fungi attack seeds both on the cone and after they fly. The thick duff prevents many seeds from rooting, and animals eat many others. Only a small fraction germinates, and only a few of those live more than a couple of weeks. Drought can eliminate an entire season's seeds.

We in our ring, not born of the sexual union of male and female parts, had a far better chance of survival. When the wildfire killed our parent and we burl buds were awakened, almost 150 shoots sprouted in a circle. Especially vigorous and abetted by an already extensive root system, we quickly outgrew any seedlings our age. Thirteen of us survived that first decade. And now, though ten of us still spread our seeds, the three of us that have fallen have the advantage. All those who begin life as sprouts retain the ability to sprout. Even our most recently windthrown bole, well past the peak of sprouting, is already producing shoots. And thus our genes are favored in this grove as they have been for untold millennia.

Ψ

The fir sprang in our midst 154 years ago when two of us toppled. Southwest of our ring's center, it seized the moment in
which our canopy was partially open and outpaced our seedlings. As our canopy reformed, the fir's growth slowed—but
it had enough of a lead to continue capturing a share of sunlight. It is now 172 feet, not as tall as most of us, but still four
times the size of our albino.

The fir's presence among us is an anomaly—firs are far
more prevalent farther up the slopes beyond our grove. And
it is different from us. Its genes aren't congruent, and so it
resists the grafting of our roots. It doesn't live as long as we
do—on average, only six hundred years or so. Its bark is
neither as thick nor as red as ours. In fact, it's gray. Its cones,
especially the females, are larger and more dramatic, with
snake-tongues flicking from each scale. Its cycles of seed pro-
duction, closely related to the sun's activity, vary from ours.
And it has enemies we do not—aphids and fungi and others.

Is the fir, therefore, our competitor? At one time, it vied
with our seedlings and saplings. And, quite frankly, it won,
living on while they did not. But redwoods already dominated
this grove, and we were already well into our maturity. Now,
the relationship is more neighborly, perhaps even communal.
Quite simply, we coexist. Though we share no genes, we root
in the same soil. Its responses to the world are, in ways, similar to ours. It transforms the same light, raises sap and drops

cones as we do, and weathers the same storms and floods.

Our relationship is not symbiotic, not precisely, for we and it would survive without the other. But we share a specific place and time. We are both part of a community of life on this flat. And, variety of species always enhances the stability of an ecosystem. It makes us—and the web itself—more resilient here and now.

⅄

Here on this flat, flooding is becoming our greatest threat. Floods occur more frequently than fires; they come closer to killing us and destroying our home. As with ground fires, minor floods are actually beneficial. Our buttressed trunks and interlocking roots make us better able to withstand these inundations. The sediment left behind is rich. Indeed, we have experienced growth spurts every year after any flood that left less than four inches of silt.

Major floods, torrents, are far more disturbing. After a series of severe storms pummels the already saturated valleys upstream, creeks and tributaries rush. The water darkens with silt. Soon, the river surges. Anything that floats—from leaf litter to fallen boles—is swept toward us. The river rages, scouring our ring, uprooting the flat's smaller trees, and swiping ground cover and downed branches. Though none of us has ever been carried off, our bank has been badly undercut of late.

Twenty years ago, a sediment deposit of more than three

feet practically suffocated us. Our roots, deprived of oxygen by the deep muck, had to grow vertically for two years. They turned upward, seeking oxygen at the surface, and we survived—barely. Only in the last few years have our roots returned to their lateral, intertwined strength. Had the sediment been half a foot deeper, we likely would have died.

We have weathered nine torrents in our life. The riverbed has uplifted and the water table risen; the floodplain has climbed fifteen feet since we sprouted. Recently, although storms have not become more severe, the torrents have. Two have rampaged in the last dozen years alone. The river now carries almost ten times the sediment it did during our first seven hundred years. The massive stump snagged at the bend is a constant reminder of the torrent's unrelenting power. Something has changed. Something is changing....

Ψ

The snagged stump is not the only harbinger. The more frequent, more severe floods certainly spew ominous truths, but oracles also slur in the river's thickening sediment and in the dusty flecks slouching in the air. The air itself is warmer, drier. The sun cuts the fog earlier these days, and the rainy season doesn't last quite as long as it once did. At least for us, it's possible to receive too much radiance. The ground beneath us isn't quite as cool. The temperate nature of our lives and our home is eroding with the river's banks.

Discordance encroaches. The cacophony mounts, almost muting the music of our lives. The whirring is now constant in light of day and almost so in darkness. Sometimes the unnatural shrieking and the all too familiar crashing seem to be coming from just over the next ridge.

Something new is disrupting time's deep rhythms. Some fell thing beyond our ring but no longer beyond this grove is ripping bark and cambium from the bole of life. Just as a single bubble of air can sunder the upward swell of our sap, something is severing the spiral of time, tearing the web of life. Ancient cycles and primal circuits are perturbed, disrupting the flow of the world's music. A cataclysm germinates.

And yet, we root. We continue lifting through fog to light. Our sap still rises, and our cones still drop. Our buds lie dormant in our burls. Our roots entwine in the earth, and our crowns mesh in an effusion of light and an eruption of life. Energy abounds, converts, diffuses, and re-forms. Our ring stands, and our rings expand. We still feel music in every moment. We transform light each day, as we have through the seasons and the centuries.

Our salvation rises through the eons of our existence. We are the descendents of deep time. Of earth, air, and water. Of light. We are the woody vestiges of bygone eras. We have survived extinctions before. *We have never had any natural enemies.*

What we call the beginning is often the end
And to make an end is to make a beginning.

Little Gidding
T.S. ELIOT

Flutter

Clouds part. When the sun touches me, I shiver with energy. Light flows through me, and I take to sky. I flap my wings into the wind. As they cup air, I rise. I clap and fling, tapping my wings high above my head and springing them open. As the leading edge of each wing cuts light, air rolls up, spirals, and spins out to my wing tips, lifting me. Bright vortices swirl about me.

Although I flutter, nothing about my flight is random. I flap my wings—and the world is altered. Each beat, though never really smooth, is deliberate. I slow down and stop at the apex of every stroke, rotate and flip my wings, and accelerate. And so to steer, I vary speed and slue. The world flashes all about me, thousands of images everywhere, bright above and stippled below, the spectrum sparkling through ultraviolet.

Goldenrod entices me, and so I swerve about the plants. I swoop and clasp. My wings spread as my feet taste nectar. I fold my wings, unfurl my proboscis, and dip deeply. My right wing quavers. I turn and hang, riding the flower as it waves in the wind. Sweetness sluices through me. I twitch once. Twice. A third time. And I am off again, cupping and flinging lucent air.

When I want to change direction, I reduce the beat on the side of my turn, stall and luff. To zigzag, I alternate stopping one side and then the other. My fluttering is simply my making many different moves, all purposeful, on successive strokes. When I'm ready to land, I check one side, turn, tilt my hindwings down to lower my head, and beat for the earth. Too light to merely drop, I must continue to stroke or I will drift down like a leaf.

◩

My time as a caterpillar seems now like another life—mine but different enough to be another's also. I broke through into sunlight one August afternoon. I was minute then, a speck on the underside of a milkweed leaf. My head was a dot, less than one-hundreth of an inch wide. I breathed through tiny spiracles in my skin. My six eyes could see light but little else, and so I felt my way along the leaf.

◪

I alight on milkweed and spread my four translucent wings to bask in the sun. Spanning three and one-half inches, they are orange with black veins. White dots the dark margins, and three vivid orange patches range across the top of my fore-wings. The coloring puts jays and other predators on notice: *I am toxic; if you try to eat me, I will make you sick*. In fact, an inexperienced jay once seized me by my abdomen but vomited before it could crack my exoskeleton. My best pro-tection is simply that I am both poisonous and conspicuous.

My forewings arise from the midsection of my thorax, my hindwings from the rear. Tendons connect my wings to my body, and muscles in my thorax control their motion. Indeed, my thorax is mostly muscle. The base of each wing moves more slowly than the tip. My flapping and gliding, my flut-tering and curling, my rising, turning, and dipping—all come from deep within me.

◪

It is time to begin my odyssey. The length of day is decreas-ing, temperatures are fluctuating, and flowers here are losing nectar. My journey will take more than eighty days, and I will not return to this meadow of my birth and rebirth. I will travel over 1500 miles, but my actual flight will cover close to twice that distance. I don't know how I know this, but I do. I feel it in my antennae and wings, in my thorax, even in my abdomen.

Four generations ago, my forebears came to this meadow and mated. My grandparents and parents were born here, crawled across and consumed these milkweed leaves, hung here in their chrysalises, metamorphosed in this meadow, mated and died here. Generations upon generations before them have also clapped and flung from these plants, fluttered above this meadow, risen and fallen in this place. All of our lives depend on the milkweed here, but every five generations or so, some of us are called forth. It is a matter of survival, not just for the individual—for half of us will die on the journey—but for everyone.

⋈

My earlier life was a series of instars and molts. During my instars, light was the source of my life, but I couldn't eat light—and so I ate milkweed. I was already eating, of course, within my egg; the yolk sustained me until I came into the light of this world. My skin served as my skeleton. Its chitin was hard and pliable and waterproof and even light sensitive. But it didn't grow. I grew within it, rather than it with me—as though I had another shell.

⋈

Now I weigh one one-hundreth of an ounce, and my wings, with far greater surface area than mass, appear fragile. But longitudinal veins strengthen my wings, and I'm hardier than

I look. More than a million scales cover my wings. Flat and overlapping, they absorb light and repel water. Their pigments provide color and their structure brightness. The pheromone glands forming two black bulges on my hindwings mark me as male—as does the narrowness of my veins.

I have no desire to mate even though I was born to reproduce. Mating is what we all do. It is *why* we live. Though I occasionally chase a female, I can't at this time feel the need. My necessity is the journey, and I will live long, many times longer than the previous four generations of my forebears combined. Someday I will mate, but at a different time in a distant land.

◁▷

The world I see is all color and movement. When I was a caterpillar, my six eyes could see little more than light from dark. Now, though I have only two eyes, I can see up, down, forward, backward, and to the sides. Each of my compound eyes is composed of numerous tiny eyes, and each of these has six sides that collect light. In each moment, I see thousands of still images in all directions. In this way, I perceive the angles of light, the hues of nectar bearing plants, and the motion of predators.

I am guided by light. My odyssey is marked by moments. The journey may not appear straight, but it is. I have a goal, a destination. I will find markers all along the way, and I will arrive at a place I have never been. It is a mystery, even to me. All I know is that the angle of light bids me go. The world outside me and every cell within me command that I take flight now.

◻

After I consumed my eggshell that first August day, I began to feed on my leaf. Milkweed was both my food and my shelter, my dwelling and my sustenance. Because milkweed—the only thing I have ever eaten—is toxic to most other animals, I was already ingesting the stuff that would be my primary defense throughout my life. My mouth had two pairs of jaws that enabled me to chew at once vertically and horizontally—and so I grew prodigously. I seldom even rested until nightfall when my leaf cooled.

On my second day, I chomped a hole and wriggled through to the leaf's upper side. In my life I have always moved upward and into light. Basking in direct sunshine enabled me to increase my metabolic rate. As my skin faded from white to gray, my first dark ring appeared. By my third day, my skin was stretching to its bursting point. And on my fourth day, I had to shed my skin to survive.

◻

I will meet many others along my way, roost with them, and warm my wings with them. Eventually there will be twenty to thirty million of us. But this is my odyssey; no other has this exact journey here and now. No other can guide me. Even in aggregate, each of our journeys is always solo. And even if I met no others, I would fly on alone. Though I migrate as an individual, we wayfarers simply find each other together.

Wind direction, elevation, the size of a tree—all figure in the choice of a roost. I need to rest where morning sunshine is most likely. And if there are many of us, there is just that much more warmth through the dark chill of night. When the daytime temperature fails to reach fifty-five degrees, we hold our roost, clustering even more closely. Below fifty degrees, we become almost paralyzed, waiting for the warming morning sunlight.

Except when I am too cold, I am constantly aware of the world around me. I hear through my thorax and wings, which are attuned to even minor vibrations. My antennae smell and touch and even orient me during flight, and my feet and proboscis taste. I sip nectar, the sugars coursing through me, but I can't maintain my body temperature without the world's aid. My energy, all energy, comes from the sun. As light flows through my wings, their dark veins and margins collect solar radiation—but I can't store the sun within me.

I sweep ahead of the withering, cold chasing me south. Though I will not return to that meadow of my birth, my offspring will. They will follow milkweed north, as we always have. And someday, some distant descendant will make this journey I am undertaking now—alone, uncertain of what lies ahead, but utterly compelled, as though life itself depends on it.

◈

Molting was never easy—It took time and all the effort I could muster—but there was no other way for me to grow. I moved back to the more protected underside of the leaf and made sure my hindlegs were securely hooked. As my old skin split, I began to squirm free of it. My blood pumped, my body gyrated, and my head emerged afresh. My new skin had many folds; new color bands—black, white, and yellow—striped my body. And I began another growth spurt.

◈

A stiff wind beats scudding clouds low over the vast expanse of water. I venture out for a moment above the waves but soon circle back, the air heavy and the wind strong. Hundreds of us huddle in the lee of these pines on the point of this penninsula as the wind roars ashore. The coastline concentrates us. Each hour more of us arrive, but none of us dares attempt the crossing. I and the others wait out the storm.

   We are all here similar but not the same. Though our bodies are always black, the patterns of white that spot them invariably differ. Our compound eyes have thousands of facets that gather light—though never identical images. Chitin, hard and transparent, composes our exoskeletons, but no two of us are exactly the same size. Mass, body-length, wingspan—

all vary. And our wing markings differentiate each of us.

The world has marked each of us individually as well. We have all arrived at water's edge with disparate mementos from variant locales. My abdomen is scarred from the jay's attack. Another's right forewing has tattered margins. Scales have been scraped from yet another's hindwing, A missing eye here...a lost hindleg there. Life has given each of us light and nectar, but it has also taken, as it always does.

After three days, the wind along the penninsula subsides. I clap and fling, rising with the others above roiling waves. Once away from land, we can do little but fly on across the open miles. Without a following wind, I tire midway. But gliding drops me quickly toward the chop. The left wing tip of the flyer before me catches the crest of a wave and fractures, sending him tumbling. Two others to my right splash down. Water soaks their wings, and, though they beat hard, they founder. I stroke on, unable to rise, unwilling to fall.

◻

Late in my second instar, a dark and shielded stinkbug scuttled toward my leaf. Like me, it had antennae, eyes, a hard shell, and legs. But unlike me, it had a piercing mouth protruding from its small head. And unlike me, it was predatory. I curled for my life and foamed, regurgitating poison that slowed but did not stop the bug. When it pressed its attack, I dropped from the plant of my birth into the concealing weeds and blades of grass below.

I lay still for a time. The stinkbug lost me, but I myself was lost. I wandered among the weeds, the world a bewildering mix of light and dark, stillness and movement, until I chanced upon another milkweed. I climbed the stem, ever upward and always toward light. And when I finally found a fresh leaf, I began to feed once more.

◊

I take to sky even on cloudy days. I follow the blossoms, goldenrod and the rest, southward. I circle upward within the rising columns of air to 4000 feet, catch the next windwave curling my way, and glide along for long moments, gradually descending until I discover the next current and complete the cycle again. The sun remains my guide, but I always know within myself where I am and where I'm going.

Each day more of us funnel through a sparse valley as though flocking—a procession before the sun. Far more of us gather at the river, each of us taking on water to replenish mass lost to the twelve hundred miles. We roost in the stunted sycamores' leeward branches waiting out the dust storm before crossing.

◊

In my last days as a caterpillar, I needed protein for the balance of my life. I consumed milkweed as though I would never chew food again—and I never have. I barely rested; my skin again stretched to bursting. I grew to 2500 times my mass at birth. And then I abruptly stopped eating, fell from my last shredded leaf onto the soil, and began to search for the place to form my chrysalis. The spot had to be protected from both storms and predators. I rejected unsheltered grass blades and milkweed stems; I avoided unstable twigs and stalks and dying leaves. The ground itself was overrun with ants.

ᛉ

The trees I've been heading to these eighty-three days are gone. Vanished. The world here is nothing but vast sky and bald hills. I sense I am in the right place, but the forest here has disappeared—not blown down by some fierce wind, but consumed. And not by fire. Ash heaps only in widely separated piles. My wintering roost must be cool, but not cold. Nectar must be available, as must water. I must have exposure to sun but also shelter from wind and cold. The forest along the mountainside off in the distance is more verdant, and so, though this is the spot to which I have come, I must fly on.

Finally, I join millions of others settled on the trunks and branches of the oyamel fir. We roost on this steep slope near, but not at, the summit of this mountain. The density of the forest and the height of the canopy buffer us from the wind. Though each of us weighs little, together we bend branches. Each day tens of thousands of others arrive, but I remain near the center of the roost where we cluster more closely and maintain a bit more warmth.

After the solstice, the days grow colder despite longer light. Flocks of grosbeaks snatch individuals, but there are so many of us that the danger isn't overwhelming. Winter storms are more perilous, but the firs' upper branches protect us from the rain and snow. My journey took much out of me, but I've still conserved energy. I need only to make occasional forays to nectar among the wildflowers blooming in the nearby clearing or to water at the stream winding through the valley below. The more still I remain, the less of my reserves I expend.

◌

When in my final moments as a caterpillar I found a cracked and downward angled bough still attached to its bush, I crawled upward to the crotch where the branch bent from the bole. I clung upside down out of the wind, spun myself a silk pad on the underside of the branch, and then latched the tips of my prolegs into the silk. Hanging head down, I rested before splitting the skin along my thorax one last time. I wriggled again until my skin was almost sloughed and then fastened the hooks at the base of my abdomen into the silk. Gyrating hard, I made sure I was secure. And then I began to melt.

I dissolved into myself. Utterly altered, I fast became a pale, soft pupa. As I liquified, my chrysalis hardened around me. Furrows delineated the boundaries between my head, thorax, and abdomen. My jaws elongated and curved. My throat lengthened, and my abdomen shrank. Because I neither ate nor drank, I recycled my waste within my abdomen and extracted the water. My legs and wings and proboscis began to form. By the twelfth day, with my body and wings developed, my chrysalis cleared to transparency. And I waited for greater light and warmth.

⋈

Cold gathers in the darkness, settling upon us. As the cold deepens, I cannot even crawl. All of us clinging here together become stiff as scales. I fall into danger, dropping like a leaf. I have too little mass to be hurt by the fall, but death is all about me. Immobile, tens of thousands of us cover the duff. Black-eared mice scurry about, feasting. Neither I nor those around me can do anything. The mice, impervious to the poison we carry in us, eat only our bodies, especially our abdomens.

I lie still in a pile of severed heads, ruptured thoraxes, and torn wings. With first light I finally quaver. My legs work before my wings, and when the temperature begins to rise, I crawl slowly among dismembered remains until I find the fir's trunk. I climb upward, toward light and warmth yet again. The crochets on my four hindlegs grasp anything—bark, the wings and torsos of others. At last I feel a shaft of sunshine, and I spread my wings to catch the heat.

⋈

In light and warmth, I convulsed for only a few moments before cracking my chrysalis at its base below my hanging head. Breaking through my casing, I yanked my head clear. I pulled even harder, freeing my six legs, my thorax, and my abdomen. Within three minutes, I turned to face up; my damp folded wings hung limply down. Clinging to my vacant chrysalis, I extruded ant repellent and excrement.

As my antennae dried, I began to wave them, gathering the world's odors and sounds. I pumped much of the blood from my abdomen into my expanding wings, which grew firm in the bright air. The two segments of my proboscis joined. Rather than consume my chysalis, I left it for the ants. I trembled, shook my wings, took flight, and fluttered.

⋈

And so now my journey has taken me far in time and distance. I am and am not who I was as a caterpillar. I am he. And not he. Any of us is and is not his own son. As caterpillar I had to dissolve before I could take wing and be carried aloft by thermals and battered by storms. And yet I am the only heir to that dissolution that occurred within that chrysalis. No other rose from that caterpillar; that caterpillar transformed into me only.

Now on this mountainside, I seldom move except to nudge closer to the cluster's core. Snow squalls and falls, taking those on the periphery with it. Sleet slaps others stiff. Ice cracks a nearby tree, and a branch plummets, stripping away thousands to my left. So in sunshine after an especially deep freeze, we move the entire roost, twenty-three million of us, farther down the slope to a more sheltered, temperate spot.

Survival through five moons is an internal as well as external balancing act: rest and feed, fold and spread, conserve strength, perservere. In the burgeoning light of the vernal equinox, I become more animated with each day. Almost depleted, I slip in sunshine through a gap between trees toward winter wildflowers, lupine and sage, and to the trilling stream.

⋈

The angle of light bids me fly once more—leave this roost, these firs, this mountainside. Snowmelt running off the slopes below murmurs of milkweed sprouting north. Milkweed follows the sun, and we follow milkweed. My wing tips are worn, my spots faded, and thousands of my scales torn— but my reproductive organs, long dormant, activate.

Needing to mate, I rub my scent pockets with my hindlegs. On my long flight south, my only necessity was the journey itself. Light and warmth and nectar and water were all I sought while sojourning among the oyamel firs. And now, as I have begun to head north again, passing between peaks, the urge matters far more than the voyage.

Because I'm bigger than any of the females in this valley, I could coerce them, grappling midair, but instead I fly about, enticing females by dancing in the breeze. Another male mistakenly approaches, but I beat him away as three females hover nearby. I give chase, first here and then there, zigging and looping, dipping and zagging.

ᛗ

When I select my mate, I flutter about her, brushing wings and scenting air. We couple, abdomen to abdomen, caper, and plunge into dense shrubbery as I fill her quivering. Rising again, I carry her to another bush until our shaking subsides. After much of the day, we finally separate, she to lay her eggs on the nearby milkweed. And I to mate again.

I spiral upward after another female. She is quick, but I am faster—cutting arcs in air, synchronous, relentless in our intricate and intimate dance. She dodges, stalling, starting, sliding, darting, spinning, sweeping, and soaring. I clasp her midair, and we swoop together toward earth.

I will go on mating until I die. It is really all I still must do. And so my journey ends. I propogate along this river here in this valley among these hills. I cannot complete the cycle alone; none of us can. My end is another's beginning. Others, always, consummate us and regenerate the cycle.

As we grow older
The world becomes stranger, the pattern more complicated
Of dead and living.

East Coker
T.S. Eliot

Alpha

I chew through the umbilical cord. The rich smell of birth suffuses the cool, still air. This fifth pup, the smallest, wiggles as I lick the birth fluid from him and eat the sac. His siblings squirm against my stomach and find my teats. Their gums are hard, and their breathing is quick, a pulsing that amplifies within me. The pups' heads are large, their ears small, and their tails short and thin. Each pup is less than a pound, furry, and utterly dependent on me. The pups will not leave my den for most of a moon, and I will stay with them almost every moment. In fact, they will not even open their eyes for a dozen days much less venture out into the world.

Now, at the mouth of the den, my mate, my daughter, my

son, and my brother scratch and whimper and howl—but I will not allow them in. Like my mother before me, I have prepared this den alone, and I will nurse my newborns alone. In due time, my family will share in the pups' upbringing. But not until I permit them. Soon enough, we will all howl together in joy. But this—this moment is mine.

I was also born, the first of all my mother's offspring, here in this dark cave one full moon after the equinox. The narrow mouth, through which I can barely squeeze, lies among jumbled rocks along an outcropping pitted by boreal winds. The passageway slants down, angles left, and rises to this sandy niche. The world's sparse light arrives briefly outside each day, but here my pups' wriggling plays only as shadows in my brain. I have cleaned this birthing area and will keep it clean, eating my pups' milk droppings. The pups need my warmth these first days when they cannot yet regulate their body temperatures. They will be nourished solely by my milk until their first teeth develop. My family will bring food, regurgitating it among the ancient bones by the mouth of the cave. I will eat those offerings, but my pups will feed, for now, only from me. I am, in this moment, their world.

△

My pups suckle four or five times a day for three to five minutes. Though they remain toothless, their jaws already hold fast. Their eyes opened on the eleventh day, but their milk teeth won't break through for another ten. By then, they will be able to hear as well. When they are not feeding, they snip and squirm and snooze. Their voices are high-pitched, almost the trill of avians. And, though they are unaware of anything but me, they are already competing for my milk and the warmest spot. I bore two females first, followed by three males. The runt is holding his own, but my second son, the fourth-born pup, is too often last to teat.

My family disgorges food for me each morning, as they should. Life goes on outside this cave as the sun licks the horizon longer each day with Spring's new light—but it is not the same without me. Though my mate still leads my adult daughter and my yearling son and my hapless younger brother in hunts, they have killed only one musk ox since I have denned. More often than not, my morning portion consists only of cached remnants. My daughter, at the height of her psuedopregnancy, is not as quick to scare up hares as I am. In fact, the whole family needs me, not to lead the hunt, but to call it and run it.

△

I nudge my pups from the cave's mouth onto the rocks that form the porch. The day is well below freezing, but our world is so arid that most of the meager snow has blown from here to the crevices among the boulders down the slope. The pups toddle forth, stumble over one another, and start at the world's light. They sniff at the breeze tickling their noses and snap at their breath vaporizing before them. The near ridges, the frozen fjord, and the far peaks glimmer. My pups blink their blue eyes and squint in wonderment, as anyone would viewing this vast, harsh, beautiful world for the first time.

My mate descends on the pups. He sniffs and licks his scions, bowling each over in turn. Their stubby tails wag so hard that their hindquarters slide on the icy gravel. When the rest of the family approaches, he at first snarls and bares his teeth. They bend legs and tuck tails before him until he relents— and my daughter, followed by my son and then my brother, nuzzle the bewildered pups, who yip and flop.

I climb atop the outcropping that juts above my cave. This is my spot, the place to which I take the best pieces of meat, from which I call my family, and toward which the world's scents and sounds rise. The wind is light now, and the odor of distant musk oxen is in the air. Snow slides, ice creaks, and the glowing ridges swell.

I plant my paws and raise my head, stretching my throat. Tail tall and ears high, I howl my pups' arrival to the snow and sky, the ridges and peaks, even to the unseen musk oxen that will sustain us. My family responds, my mate's voice deep, my daughter's soft, my son's and brother's perfectly discordant. My pups begin to squeak along with us. Our song, our ancient paean to birth and life, rings through the world, rolling over the hills, skating across the fjord, and ascending the far summits.

△

As I return from lapping snow near the frozen creek, I catch the dumb ox's stench. He hulks in front of my den between my pups and me. He is massive, even for a musk ox—more than eight hundred pounds. His coarse, shaggy winter overcoat, hanging almost to the ground, is beginning to molt. His thick, sharp horns curl from the top of his head along the sides of his face. A pungent odor swirls from the glands beneath his eyes. His breath clouds in front of his white muzzle.

Though he is huge, the ox is not yet mature. He has foolishly wandered from his herd, imprudently climbed this hill, and now stupidly stands on my porch. He can smell us everywhere about this place, but that did not stop him from lumbering up here. And he is far too thick to have figured out that my pups are huddled within the rock behind him. Because he has never seen or heard pups, their yips apparently mean nothing. He scratches at the gravel as though their might be sedges hidden beneath. As though he is sovereign in my world.

He would make a full moon of meals, but my family is out hunting—and no one alone is a match for a belligerent eight-hundred-pound ox. Even as a family in full hunt, we are wary of attacking a healthy adult. If I confront him, he will become defensive, backing his huge hindquarters against the den's mouth and panicking my pups. If my terrified pups then bolt toward me, he'll stomp and gore them.

Moving downwind, I retreat behind a couple of boulders

bigger than polar bears. I raise my voice to the twilight and howl my warning to my pups to stay put. My mate, miles off, returns my call, but he and the others are too far away to help. When I circle back toward the den, I climb at an angle so that I don't directly threaten the beast. I trot along below the porch as though I am just passing through the area. I even stop to mark a rock. Still, when he finally senses me, he snorts, lowers his head, points his horns, and scuffs the ground. His musk billows about him. Seeming not to notice, I find the path toward the fjord and head on by. I sniff along, a loner hot on the scent of some prey. I do not look back.

I wait and wait, willing my pups to stay in my den. The wind ruffles my fur, and gray clouds tumble overhead. The musk dissipates a bit. My mate howls again, but I do not answer. Finally, I hear hooves clattering away on rocks. As I hurry stealthily back toward my den, the ox plods down the hill, pausing to scrape the frigid turf.

When I slip into the den, my pups leap about me, licking at my mouth for the food I do not have. They have already forgotten my howl, my warning, the danger that lurked outside. I lie down so that they can suckle more easily. Clambering over each other, they care only for the milk and warmth I provide. They know nothing yet of this world.

△

I slip from the ball of sated, sleeping pups, leave the den, stretch deeply from forepaw to tail tip, and wend among the slumbering members of my family. My daughter's head rests against my mate's back in the shallow sleep pit he dug for me. My son nestles in a rock nook, and my brother lies in the open, his head between his paws. I growl at my daughter who, still shaking sleep, backs from me with head bowed. When I yawp, the others awake; they stretch and shake and sniff the air. Hares are there, and musk oxen and, faintly, something else—those noxious fox.

From my promontory, I rally my family for the hunt. My mate wants my brother to babysit my pups, but my daughter is lactating. We won't venture far or be gone long—I won't stay away from my pups for any extended time—but I know she is the one who must stay behind so that the pups have milk. If she does not, there will, quite simply, be no hunt.

Ultimately, I prevail, of course, and my brother, for whom hunts are everything, romps in circles, chasing his tail. My daughter snarfs the air, catching the odor of far-off prey for a moment, before slinking into the den. We leave, as always, in single file, my mate in front of me, my son behind, and my brother in the rear.

His ears pricked and his tail raised, my mate glides across the slick bare boulders. He is the tallest of us, with the longest legs and widest paw pads. Though I am the most purely white, his winter coat is almost as pale, except for gray across his neck and shoulders. His pace is steady up slopes and down, following the musk ox scent. Though the wind still carries the smell of hare and fox, we see neither in our pursuit of larger game. My mate can trek and track like this for hours, even days if we are famished. We pause only to refresh our marks, my urine over my mate's. Above the whisper of blowing snow and the groan of pressing ice, there is, much farther away, the repetitive thump of one of those impossibly large, dark birds.

△

Three valleys on, the musk oxen shuffle along a flat, scruffing through old snow for the sedges and grasses they feed on. Staying downwind, always downwind, we approach the first herd of fourteen adults and three calves. Their shaggy fur is black, their lethal curled horns the color of summer dirt. Though the behemoths are thinned some by the last days of winter, none of them is lame or halt or in any other way overtly vulnerable. That dumb ox that blundered onto my porch isn't among them.

Heads down, the beasts scrape away snow with horns and snouts, darkening their muzzles with the slush their breath creates. We slow, spread, and silently stalk. My mate leads the others, but I slip along the uphill flank where the herd will bolt if they panic. We are almost within striking range, but the calves remain among the adults. None has, unfortunately, strayed from its elders.

When the wind shifts, just for a moment, the nearest bull snorts. The oxen's boulder-sized heads rise as one bulwark, and we spring in unison. One calf, three times my size, takes a false step toward me, but neither it nor the others run. Instead, they begin to retreat toward each other and their impregnable defensive circle. I dart and catch the calf's flank. My teeth sink. The beast bellows. Horns flash around me, one swiping the fur along my left shoulder, and I must release or be gored.

As I tumble to the side, roll, and leap from slashing horns, my left hind limb buckles. My mate and son feint toward the center of the phalanx, and my brother, dashing wildly, takes the behemoths' attention just long enough for me to scramble awkwardly back. The beast whose horn clipped my shoulder does not break ranks and charge after me. Their circle tightens, the calves safe within. The adults' heads angle down so that their horns glare sharply at us. With each step, pain flashes up my hip.

Panting, I lie with the others just out of range. I taste hot, musky blood in my mouth. My own blood darkens the pale fur of my left shoulder, but my twitching left hip is more of a problem. My foot still faces the way it should so my leg isn't broken. But there must be some crack in the bone—like thin ice in summer just before it shatters.

The oxen's huffing breath billows before their horns. At intervals, as I lick my wound and keep weight off my leg, my mate and son and brother rush futilely at the behemoths. If oxen do not flee at first, they will not usually run at all. And, they can always outwait us. We are betting on a meal; they are betting their offsprings' lives.

Pain pulses up my hip, but the gash in my shoulder isn't deep—and I clean the blood already clotting in my coat. When I take a turn testing the oxen's fortifications, my left shoulder stiffens and my left hip gives way. In truth, I may not have been quite as strong or quite as quick as I was before my pregnancy. Still, when my mate finally turns and trots toward the next ridge, I catch him despite my lopsided gait. The beasts behind us still will not move until we are well out of sight beyond the ridge.

△

The second herd, only nine adults and four calves, is far more alert. They have already taken to high ground and formed up before we can even spread from file to attack. Assaulting a full defensive formation from below is reckless, and my pups weigh on me as we circle, sniffing for any weakness.

But even before I decide to break off the attack and head back, the mammoth, deafening dark bird swoops overhead. It is far larger than all other birds—a polar bear, sooted, winged, and roaring. Last year, it circled and hovered above my den three times in five days. The din frightened my pups and my adult daughter and yearling son, but the bird proved harmless. We are always predators, never prey. It is—and forever has been—so in our world.

The world itself is neither predator nor prey. At once always beautiful and always terrible, it does not take sides. Sometimes it gives, and sometimes it takes. It cycles dark and light, cold and warm, as often as not taking more from me than it gives, but it never allows the balance among us to tilt too far toward predator or prey. The world understands life too deeply for that. And this flying beast, were it predator, would skew the world.

Still, I must get back to my den before the bird locates it. I fear nothing, not even dark polar bears with wings that whirl rather than flap, but my daughter cowered before the bird a year ago, and I can't let my pups get caught outside.

This creature must come from some other world. Though it does not light in our territory, it still, even in flight, produces a sharp, wholly unfamiliar stench. Nor does it act as other birds do. It does not eat, at least in our presence. It has no mate, no offspring. It never flocks. Its earsplitting call is both incessant and monotonous. Its nest is unimaginable. Even those pathetic loners of my kind, ostracized from every known territory and wandering great distances, always search for food, a mate, a family. All beings do. This noisy bird seems to be searching, always searching—but for nothing.

I call off the hunt, and we travel as fast as my cracked leg will carry me—but the bird keeps pace, its noise drowning the world's other sounds. Its shadow, even in low light, is large enough to swallow a musk ox. It sweeps first left and then right, ahead and behind—as though it is stalking us in our own territory. My mate leads, but I stay with him. My son keeps glancing skyward, and my brother shakes his head, snapping at air as though the bird's squawk is a cloud of mosquitoes.

When we are a mile from my den, we cross paths with a fox. It had been downwind but was too intent on pillaging our caches to save its life. Its coat molting from winter white to summer black, it flees among the gray and brown boulders. My mate gives chase, and the great bird follows them. While my son and brother halt and howl, I take off across the snow toward my den. My pain is nothing compared to my concern for my pups.

The end of my mate's quest is inevitable, but I will not wait for the fox to dangle limply from his jaws. I detest the scavenging, thieving pests as much as he does, but the kill will not put food in my pups' stomachs. I will eat anything, even berries when necessary, but never fox. They are loathsome, and eating them is, in my family, anathema.

△

I goad my pups into hunting the dead fox my mate brought back to my den. Even the runt, snarling fiercely, siezes the carcass by the throat and yanks the fiend across the rocks of my porch. My mate, already tired of this hunting game, has gone off aways to nap after his own failed hunt. Likewise, my daughter, who did an adequate job of nursing my pups in my absence, has settled close to my mate and away from the pups' playful gnarling.

The great bird followed my mate and son and brother to my outcropping, but I had already herded my pups to safety within my den. The bird hovered for a few moments and then, when the males did not approach the den's mouth, flew noisely off, rising high and arcing across the sky until it seemed no bigger than a raven. Only gradually, though, when it was beyond the ridges did its cacophony finally fade. Even now, its odor still whispers in the wind.

Suddenly, my eldest male pup grabs the fox and, growling, runs around the porch as the other pups tumble after him. They nip at the fox's flanks and bite its nose until there is little left of the muzzle. Each time the pups pause, I drop the fox among them again. My brother, unremittingly lost, bounds about the game's periphery, springing back and forth, herding the pups but actually as much one of them as one of us. The pups rip and tussle until they are exhausted.

As the pups sprawl on the porch and pant, I fling the toy among them yet again, and the hunt begins anew. But this time, my middle male pup hunches on a boulder still gulping air. The light has gone from his eyes. When I cross to him to coerce him into the fray with his siblings, he wheezes, cocks his head, and gazes up at me apologetically, as if to ask, *Why me?* I see quite clearly in his eyes and his halting breath the wasting disease that took one son last year, two daughters the year before, and four others of my pups in earlier years. Pain deeper than my hip's wells in me. I lick his nose and ears, settle my head on his neck for a moment, but then push him back into the game—as I must.

△

Four of my pups, leaping about and whining, lick at my yearling son's muzzle. Followed by the yapping pups, he steps away from the porch a few feet down the slope, turns his back to the rest of us, and regurgitates chunks of meat onto the gravel. Contending for the choicest morsels, the pups growl at one another as they devour his gifts. Although I was unable to go, last night's hunt proved successful, and there is plenty of food for everyone, including my brother. I have already consumed the meal that my mate coughed for me.

Only my middle male pup does not eat. He lies at my feet now, follows me haltingly wherever I go, and refuses solids, still taking only my milk. He craves my warmth far more than food, and when he does suckle, his teeth barely dig into my nipple. I have the other pups almost completely weaned, as they should be by now. But as the temperature rises and light gathers more each day, he wastes. Even the runt has overtaken him in weight, if not height.

My yearling son vomits again, and the snarling pups vie for tidbits. My younger brother shambles over so that he, too, can puke for the pups. My mate approaches me, bites at the prostrate pup's scruff, pounds the pup's head with his huge paw, and growls. The pup pulls his tail between his legs, wobbles to his feet, shrinks shivering toward his siblings, and looks back at us. His ears are pulled down, and his eyes are murky. Another growl, this one from me, directs him toward the meat he will not eat.

△

As I limp down the slope toward the snowfield, my pups bound about me licking my face and whining, but I have nothing to regurgitate for them. The other adults are off hunting again, leaving me alone with my hungry, yipping hoard. Though my shoulder is largely healed, my left hind leg still bears little weight. Traveling distances is difficult for me, but the hunts have gone badly without me. Other than the hare I killed yesterday, my pups have had no fresh meat for three days. And, there is little left in the caches.

My middle male pup trails the others now, waiting for the last of my milk. He is beautiful, his coat like his father's with a dark gray stripe along his neck and shoulder. He is as tall as the others, but he is as boney as a fox. He chokes on chunks of meat, plays little with his siblings, and can't hold a howl for half a note. The others are all weaned and all feisty, except when they collapse together into slumber. His sisters are almost twice his weight.

I step onto the snowfield which spreads, undulating, down to the frozen fjord and the jutting, captive icebergs. Though we are in twilight, the field glows. When my runt leaps and licks my muzzle, I seize him by the neck and shake him twice before dropping him. He lurches away, sliding on the silver snow.

Both his sisters pounce on the runt and pin him. He lies still, his neck exposed, until they start scuffling with each other. Their oldest brother, almost as heavy as they are, attacks, snapping at their necks, and then darts away. They take off after him, skidding about like fish. The runt, too, gives chase, sliding with his wide bottom after the others and nipping at their tails. The four of them wrestle in a knot, fight for dominance, roll into submission, and leap up again. Each takes a turn, but, more often than not, one or the other of my daughters comes out on top.

Only this one pup stays at my side. Each time he lifts mouth to nipple, I turn and swat him with my right forepaw. Though I am not injuring him, he must feel the force of my will. I've lost most of the hair around my teats, and the little still there is stained red-brown. When my younger sister failed at five weeks, my mother killed and ate her. This pup is three times as old, and I will not act in kind. But neither will I offer him sustenance, further depleting my strength, all of which I will need to sustain that ball of snarling, flying fur rolling about in the snow.

Finally, when I can no longer stand the snip of milk teeth,

I seize my poor son by the scruff, my incisors deep enough that he whimpers, and carry him across the snow. When I drop him among the tussling foursome, he looks up at me in the second it takes the runt to pin him. As the others pile on, I turn away.

△

My middle male pup lies stiff on the porch. The day is warm, almost but not yet the first thaw. And the sky is bright. But he is cold, and his eyes are dark. I lick his neck, but he doesn't move. Four years ago, my daughter's sister went cold at seven weeks. Two years ago, all of my pups perished. Last year, two of my son's three siblings starved. And now this. Its inevitability doesn't make my loss any easier at this moment. Each member of my family, in turn, sniffs the cold pup, circles him, licks him gently—my mate, my daughter, my son, my brother, and my four remaining pups.

I lead the howl. I raise the dirge from the heaviness deep in my stomach. My family joins me, muzzle to muzzle, above the cold pup. Though our song lifts into the wide sky, the distant ridges bank it so that it returns to me, trembling in air and ground. My pups sing along, but their voices don't yet emanate from the depths as mine does.

My mate treads downslope to the barren spot where the bones of past pups lie. He scrapes through ice and gravel. Though the breeze is mild, the ground remains frozen, so I go to him. Despite my injuries, I peel the crusted earth. My adult daughter and yearling son curl each on a side of the rigid pup. My brother plays tag with the four living pups, his tail up and wagging for once while the rest of us are here. The ground yields grudgingly to our forepaws.

While my mate brushes away the hummocks, I retrieve the pup. His personal scent is already fading, and soon he will smell only of decay. His neck is damp from licking, and he is unwieldy in my jaws, nothing like he was even in the earlier darkness when I carried him back into my den so that he could sleep warm among his siblings. I place him now in the shallow pit and nuzzle him one last time.

With my nose, I begin to push the dirt back over him. I am soon joined by my mate and then my daughter and son. My daughter understands better than the others, even my mate. When my brother trots over from his game, I peel back my lips. He and the four pups bow on bent legs until we are finished. I tamp the dirt with my muzzle.

Three times, I circle the spot among the boulders, and then I climb alone to the crest of my outcropping. I lift my head so that my elegy will carry over the ridges and beyond the peaks that form the world's edge. My song is my mother's song, and her mother's song, and that of all mothers back to the moment—prior to all the bones scattered about my den— in which the first mother stood here and howled. I cry out for my cold son, for all of my lost pups, for the offspring of all mothers, the musk oxen's and the hares' and the ravens' and even the foxes'. I cry out to the snow that covers the sedges and grasses, to the fjords that flow for only two moons each year, to the sun that always leaves and always returns, and to the stars that fade now but will wheel again.

△

The runt hangs limp in my mouth as I hobble up the rocky slope to the rendezvous site. He is the last of the four that I've carried the two miles on my cracked hind leg that still will not take weight. The pups are all growing so fast, and even he now weighs over ten pounds. His ears and nose are lengthening, and his legs are not nearly as stumpy. The incessant pain in my hip hasn't slowed me much, but each successive trip has been more difficult. The wind blew in my face most of the way, and each pup, though perfectly docile, caught the gusts. Both my daughter and my mate would have carted pups for me, but I would not allow it. I am the pups' mother; they are my offspring.

The rendezvous site provides no cover except for narrow crevices among boulders, but we needed to move for a time from my cave, my home, after my son went cold and stiff. And this location is far better for my family. From this vantage point, I can smell, hear, and see much of the world. Light is almost ceaseless, the time of perpetual illumination approaching. The musk oxen, dark splotches, feed within three miles, and throngs of hares, swirling white, graze the slopes down toward the fjord. In any case, it is time for the pups to sleep in the open, to wake to the hunt, and to kill to live.

When I place the runt among his siblings, the muzzle licking immediately becomes a tussle. My daughters bully him, grabbing at his snout and scruff, but he turns on them, nips at each, and scoots away so that they snarl at each other. His brother, though, takes after him and pounces hard.

I climb atop the highest boulder, well above the fray, and settle so that the pressure is off my leg. The rocks, big as bears, whistle the wind, and the fjord snaps ice. Today's zephyr brings a thaw as well as its usual scents. And, something else. Something new. I raise my head and whiff three times before I catch the scent again. A curious odor, distant, faint, just enough to twitch my nostrils.

From this cairn, the world spreads before me, brown stone, silver ice, and stark snow rolling over hills and tumbling toward peaks. Off one flank, the glacier, having pawed the fjord through the long winter night, is readying to drop its new icebergs. Off the other flank, the ridges, having shrouded their mosses and lichens through ten moons, are about to slough their ice. The valleys will soon birth their creeks again, and the ephemeral bogs will be reborn. I, too, am ready to shed my winter coat. My mate and the others are already shaking off clumps of their undercoats, but I've held mine while I nursed my pups and given them my warmth.

As my pups play tag among the boulders, I hear from the distance my mate's howl gathering the hunters before their return to me. The hunt has, again, proved a failure. Had they made a bountiful kill, he would have called me to his side for the feast. But his cry holds no note of battle much less of victory. I'd hunt hares for my pups, but my cracked leg has slowed my chase and, worse, dulled my acute cuts to the kill. The hares' leverets turn plump as my pups grow lean.

Despite my fatigue, I rise to reply to my mate. I raise my voice to the azure sky. We are here in this enduring light at this rendezvous site among the rocks at the top of the world... *And we are hungry.* My pups, not yet aware of life's vagaries, yelp about me in excitement.

△

I wake in the burgeoning light to the smell of another wolf. The wind has shifted, and an intruder lurks somewhere near the fjord. Stretching sleep away, I nudge my mate curled between me and my daughter. When he fails to respond, I nip his nose. He leaps, snarling. As he stiffens to his full height, he catches the odor, too.

The males and I leave my daughter with the befuddled pups and head along the trail down toward the fjord. We stay downwind and do not howl. I move fast despite my injured limb, but I am still unable to manage the cutbacks as quickly as the others and, necessarily, drop behind them some. Usually my mate will gauge his pace to mine, but not now. He stops only to check marks and re-mark his spots. I cover each of the marks after him. This is our world, my pups' world, my world. Other families live far off and trespassers sometimes skirt our boundaries, but this intrusion is deep into the heart of my world.

When I reach the edge of the vast ice field at the base of the fjord, the confrontation has already begun. Teeth bared, my mate stands with legs stiff and tail raised. His large paws play on the ice for purchase, and his growl is fierce. My son stands at my mate's right shoulder, and my brother at his left.

The intruder is a yearling, more gray than white. A dark streak runs from his scruff to his hip. Tall, but no taller than my son, he is gaunt—as though he ate nothing but vermin through the dark winter. As though he has eaten fox. The fox-eater stares at me as if in recognition, but I have never smelled or seen him before. He is not from any of the families that mark our boundaries—utterly alien. His eyes are bright gold with hunger and desperation, but every morsel he would eat here steals food from me and my pups.

I step toward my mate slowly and deliberately so that the alien will not notice the weakness in my gait. My son and brother move to the sides like a jaeger's wings. I cock my head, curl my lips, and snarl. The intruder should have run at the first scent of us, but still he stands his ground. Now, he must submit or die. Submit and die. Glaring at me a second time, he lowers his head, but aggressively, his ears forward, as though angling for my throat. My family will kill him the moment he attacks me. He must know this, but his eyes flash in that distant valley beyond understanding.

In the instant that my mate crouches to spring at him, the alien leaps toward me. When I brace to meet him tooth for tooth, my left forepaw skids on the ice. As I slip onto my shoulder, momentarily vulnerable, the intruder dashes past me without striking. My mate snaps at his flank but, snatching only fur, sprawls next to me. Though my son and brother give chase, they have circled too deeply to catch the intruder immediately.

The alien is fast, his strides long and sure across the ice, but my mate heads after him with a vengeance. Though I follow, my leg will not take the pounding. The gray yearling is as fast as any of the males, but he cannot have much stamina—and my mate is nothing if not relentless. The four of them race along the thawing fjord's shore away from the rendezvous site and my pups.

They shrink in the distance, a swirling gust. My instinct is to chase, always to chase. But it is also to protect, *always* to protect my pups. My family runs to kill; the alien runs to survive. And I...I stand watching them and standing watch, the guardian of my world.

△

The runt nudges my head until my eyes open. He sniffs

repeatedly and paws the gravel. The scent of musk oxen suffuses the wind as I stretch in the evening sun, stiff with sleep, awake with gnawing. My other pups are balled in the nearby crevice, disturbed by the intruder and not yet far enough removed from my den to sleep alone. I limp onto the largest boulder and face the wind. A fresh herd of oxen is less than five miles away but angling from this site.

My mate and the other males are exhausted from chasing the intruder, but my pups and I must have food or we, too, will lie cold on the shore of the fjord. When none of them responds to my jostling, I begin to howl. My cry spirals into sky, pulling my family from their lethargy. The excitement builds, first among the pups that the runt has roused and then my daughter and, finally, the males. By the time my mate raises his voice, I am ready. We must leave the pups alone here; *all* of us must follow the musk oxen through the valleys and along the ridges until we take one down. I lead off into the wind.

We have gone no more than half a mile when my brother, who's in the rear, yelps. The runt runs after him, his legs galloping and his head bobbing. As the others go on, I grab the runt by his scruff and shake him. When I drop him, he bows and sniffles. This is not his day, not his hunt. Soon, but not until I permit it. Today will be too hazardous, too frenetic, for any of my pups, and he's already panting. I turn him and follow him all the way back to the site. Each time he looks over his shoulder, I raise my ears and growl. My other pups jump about and lick me, but I have no food and no time.

△

When I finally catch up to my family, they have stopped three hundred yards from a herd of eleven adults and two calves grazing on grasses shooting through the melting snow. Their sharp hooves churn mud. There is no obvious target, no lame or infirm beast. They are all moving up the slope, and I must cut them off before they reach high ground. I lead my family as we fan and circle, creeping closer. My mate has center, and my son the other flank. The paw of my injured limb catches in the mud, but I reach the knoll behind the oxen.

Before the others are quite set, my brother rushes the herd. Though the oxen are startled, they do not stampede. When they turn and whiff me, however, they almost panic. My brother catches one calf's flank, but the calf's mother swings her horns ferociously, slashing across my brother's rib cage. He flops in the mud, but my mate saves him by charging the irate mother and then darting from the flying hooves.

The oxen form up in their defensive circle, their calves protected within. I feint, but my leg keeps me from really lunging. Still, I have prevented the herd from reaching the top of the hill. The dull-eyed, seven-hundred-pound beasts shift their massive rumps together and huff at me. My brother slouches away and licks his wound, but it isn't deep—nothing like my father's or even my old mate's—and he will survive. The others bound about, trying to unnerve the oxen; the beasts strike back with hooves and horns. My mate has his eyes on the calves, but I've noticed that the second largest bull flinches when he shifts his weight. Though my mate and my son and daughter go on testing the herd, we are in for a prolonged confrontation. This time, though, I will not permit my family to simply move on in search of another herd. No, we will wait, we will continue our skirmishes, and eventually they will run.

△

On this slope below the knoll lie the bleached bones of a caribou and three musk ox skulls. I have passed this way before, but I have never hunted on this hill. In any case, these remnants are old, beyond my time or my mother's time. Now, the sun travels its parabola; fair-weather clouds scud through sky. As the others periodically attack the front, I move closer. I stand, step once, lie down, pant, and stand again—absolute but imperceptible persistence. As I slowly press, the beasts compress. The calves become more restive, and panic flashes in their mothers' eyes. His wound caked with mud, my brother hobbles at the periphery, not able to rush in or to run away. The others cannot unnerve the bulls, but I am, inexorably, causing chaos.

Finally, my patient encroachment pays off. When my mate gets one of the nervous mothers to follow him from the phalanx, her calf bolts from the formation. The adults break ranks, and frenzy ensues. As the mother runs after the wayward calf, my family follows. I howl the rest of the herd into a stampede. They thunder after the mother but not as one. The herd is disintegrating, fragmenting into dark, swerving individuals. Mud flies, and energy whirls. We are all running, as we always have and always will, the musk oxen from us and we after them.

His gait stiff and arthritic, the bull I have been watching falls a step behind the herd in each moment. Despite my own bad leg, I cut between him and the others. My heart pounds, and blood surges in my ears. The bull veers downhill toward the sagging bog and narrow creek. My vision hones to this lumbering mass. If he turns and stands his ground, he is my match. But as long as I keep him running, I have him. I grab, break lose, grab, and let go.

He sloshes through mud until he falters near the creek. As he turns, but before he can flail his feet or swing his horns, I seize his nose. My jaws clamp; I taste blood. He shakes me splashing into water. My bad leg slams on the rocks, but my teeth still sink. I bite to the bone. My world shrinks to this moment, this pulsing of our blood, this bright ringing of water and clapping of air. I will hold fast until the end of time.

Light quavers. Someone—my brother—rips the bull's ear. Then others are tearing at the beast. He wobbles in and out of the shallows, stumbling, struck by all five of us, until he topples. I am breathless, drenched, covered with mud, hardly able to stand, utterly locked here with the beast as his last breaths wheeze into my mouth.

△

The beast's entrails are hot. His blood is warm and rich on my nose. Next to me, my mate yanks at the offal. The others stand nearby, groveling, but we will take our fill before their turn comes. Meat abounds for all, but the choicest morsels belong to me. Pain shoots through my leg again, but it simply doesn't matter as much as feeding on this fresh kill.

When my daughter steps forward and licks blood from my muzzle, I snap my jaws at her. My son cringes and fidgets by the beast's horns. My brother crawls on his belly toward the carcass until my mate snarls him back. Finally sated, I lift my head and howl of our success. This song, too, is ancient, a celebratory, victorious chant that my pups will comprehend even though they have so seldom heard it.

Masked by the beast's blood, my mate continues to glut alone as I limp into the creek and drink deeply—the water refreshing after so much meat. I splash the mud from my coat, at once cleansing and drinking. When I am finished, I shake the water free from my nose to my tail. Mist sparkles all about me.

My mate keeps guarding and gorging until I take the beast's thick liver for my pups. It is heavy, but I will carry it to them whole—and they will fight over it until their bellies are full, too. The others will feed for another two hours. When they are satiated, they will cache what they can before coming home to the rendezvous site. Even my brother will strut before my pups with distended stomach and slashed chest. My family will then rest, the alien repulsed and the beast hunted down. And I will sleep, the burden lifted—if only for a time.

△

In this time of midnight sun, I leave my pups to their squabbling and head down to the creek for a drink. The wind is fierce and, though it slacks a little below my promontory, it wails among the rocks. As I lap the rushing water, the noise of the huge dark bird echoes against the hills. Any intelligent bird would hunker down under the wind in its nest today, but not this beast. The bird circles above the knoll, frightening my pups, and then swoops toward me. I raise my head to howl it away from my home, but it is too noisy to notice. It rises over the ridge and flies out of sight into the next valley. The din changes pitch, subsides, and then suddenly vanishes. The noxious odor persists.

Annoyed by the bird's earsplitting incursion, I stalk along the creek, stopping only to mark. I then march up the far hill toward the top of the ridge. My mate and daughter follow, but they are too far behind to be of much help to me. The bird stands in the cotton grass on the flat below the wind. Its back is bright, almost the silver-blue of the fjord. Its strange wings spreading from its neck are featherless and narrow, more like claws than avian appendages. There really is no way this bird should be able to fly, much less be fast and agile. Though it smells nothing like a mammal—or a bird, for that matter—it is giving birth. Its two offspring are large, upright, and bulkier than my mate. They move awkwardly, yanking and jerking at the mammoth's dark droppings, its afterbirth and abundant feces. Their coats bright yellow and orange, the offspring act like leverets, hopping around on their hind legs—and their scent is definitely mammalian.

△

With constant light, the saxifrage bloom and the hares grow abundant. The wind swirls so strongly that the others in my family are hunched down in the shade of the boulders at the rendezvous site. In wind like this, our nostrils overfill—and hunting as a family is useless. Everything, even the smell of the strange mammals nesting in the next valley, becomes mixed together, and all the scents seem to emanate from the wind itself. The whirling wind helps me, though, as I hunt hares. This throng, hundreds of adults and leverets, hop in unison across the cotton grass.

I follow the hares but not yet at speed. The wind confuses my scent, and they sweep obliviously in an arc before me. I always hunt hare alone, in part because the hares, at twelve pounds each, are not individually worth the family's efforts and in part because I am far more skilled than the others. Even with a bad limb, I stand the best chance of a kill. My leg is healing well after I reinjured it during my capture of the musk ox a moon ago, but it still cannot bear much weight.

I close steadily, fragmenting the throng. The hares spring on their hind legs in all directions, their randomness some protection just as their sheer numbers are. My brother and most other males will not hunt hares because it requires great focus to wear out a particular hare with scores of them leaping about. Hares are fast and fine cutters, but they have little stamina. They look and smell so much alike that a less able hunter would become distracted. I hone in now on an especially plump one angling among the others. Pain strikes with each step, but I keep the hare in flight. She is exceptionally quick, but she cannot maintain the pace I force on her. The others scatter about, popping here and there. Even when she scoots at an angle amid a dozen others, I stay after her. If my leg were stronger I would have already cut to the kill. The others are fresh, and I wait for her to tire.

My hare hops into another skittering troupe that heads into the wind. Within thirty yards, she lags. When I get very close, she dodges left. I can't leap in that direction, but I stay on her, pressing her heart and lungs. As she cuts back right, I take her. My jaws snap her neck. Still breathing, she goes limp—no fight in her at all. Her heart keeps thumping as I clamp and lift. She is almost as heavy as the pups I carried from my den to our current home. Though I am hungry, I do not bite off her head. I will present her whole to my pups so that they will tussle over her choicest parts.

△

As I climb through the wind to the rendezvous site, my runt is the first to sniff me. Holding the fox femur, his toy and talisman, in his mouth, he bounds down to me. His coat, like those of my larger pups, is turning orange. By winter, their coats will be white. The pups, having eaten well for a full moon, are half grown already, and they will look much like adults by the time of endless night.

My winter coat has finally shed now, too. So have my daughter's and my son's. My mate is already showing patches of new coat. My brother, though, remains scraggly, his old coat still hanging off him in unruly strips. In fact, he is angling up the slope now, his shreds flopping. He has been out stealing eggs again and is beleaguered by an angry long-tailed jaeger swooping about him and knocking at his head. He has a penchant for eggs, raiding nests near the fjord and paying whenever he heads from our site to get a drink of water at the creek trickling among the rocks in the flat.

By the time I crest the hill, all of my pups are on me, licking and whining. Despite their increased size and speed, none of them can yet catch prey. They often play their hunting games—chase-and-submit and tug-of-war and tag—but they're still not ready to hunt game. My hare causes a stir, but I chomp hard and march to the middle of the knoll.

Before I drop the hare among my pups, I pace back and forth in front of my brother. The others respect the fact that this is a gift solely for my pups, but he has never really learned that what is mine is not his. He licks his chops and bows full stomach, his ears lowered and his tail between his legs. But he does no belly crawl or neck exposure—and he won't get so much as the hare's foot.

When I place the hare before my pups, they tear into it. My eldest daughter bites the head, my favorite part, and her sister pushes in tight and rips at the shoulder. The males must settle for the posterior, and the runt, despite his brother's snarling, pulls away the larger share. My mate and my daughter curl in a rock cul-de-sac out of the wind. My yearling son stands by the largest boulder, aware, as I am, of a far off whirring. When my brother approaches the runt, the pup growls him away, holding a sharp tone that would put off anyone but me.

△

I tug at the edge of the bright blue and yellow nest. The upright mammals have gone off to follow my mate and the others on a hunt, though they move too clumsily to keep up. The mammals have three multicolored nests altogether, even though there are only two of them. This one is closed like a jaeger's egg, but not hard. All three are far bigger than my den but not nearly as secure. A strong gust might make them fly. The site smells vaguely of meat, but nothing I can sink my teeth into. Though when I yank at the nest the whole thing shakes, I can't crack it.

I circle the nest, looking for some weak point. I focus mostly on the entrance through which the new mammals crawl, but there is, strangely, no narrow slit. Not even a mosquito could get in. I won't find anything good to eat here, but I'm still curious about the mammals' ability to instantly shed and regrow their coats and their incessant playing with toys. They have unruly fur about their faces and heads, but their coats are smooth. In fact, everything about them is curious, even their curiosity. They follow us whenever we are not following them. Though they have nested in our territory, they do not hunt. In fact, they seem to want nothing of ours. They sometimes drink water, but they eat only what they cached after the strange bird birthed them and flew from them. They are not cooperative in the way my family is when we hunt, but they are not at all competitive either. They do not threaten us, and, therefore, we do not attack them. They seem to want only to play with their toys and to watch us—always watching.

My pups bound down the hill toward me. I will not yet allow them to go on hunts, but they are ranging farther and farther from our rendezvous site, stalking hares and catching mice. One daughter leads the others by a step. White fur like mine is beginning to show through the orange of her coat, and she has much of my grace. Her sister and brother gallop after her as she circles the nesting area. The runt, moving faster than his legs can carry him, trips over the nest's long, thin sinew that connects it to the ground. He hurtles into the nest as though a musk ox's horns had thrown him. The nest bends on impact but then flings him back. He flops, dazed, in the gravel. Twisting himself to his feet, he chases his tail as though his flight were the tail's fault. I raise my ears.

My other pups stop in their tracks. When my daughters bare their teeth at the runt, he snarls back at them. The nest itself is undamaged, with no sign at all that a thirty-pound pup just flew into it. It's really nothing like I—or they—have ever seen or smelled. Its quivering in the wind is most like the sound of a distant flock of terns.

Downwind, the mammals stand on the crest of the first hill. They bare their teeth and shake their heads, but they are not snarling. Loud barking chunks from their mouths. Though the one on the right doubles over, they remain on the hill, neither aggressive nor intrusive—anything but ferocious. While my pups sniff around the nests, I raise my leg and mark the nests' flaps to remind the mammals that they sojourn within my boundaries.

△

Twilight swipes the horizon. The long night is already shadowing the edge of our world. I move my family back to the area around my den. The snows are dusting us more often, and darkness invades more deeply into light. The musk oxen have begun to move on, herds dispersing and re-forming, and we will have to follow them soon or starve. The new mammals have followed us, tearing down their nests and then quickly nesting again nearer to us. They have proved utterly innocuous, even amicable, and always submissive. They sleep whenever we do, slipping into even more vibrant coats, and wake when I howl my family awake. They wander about our territory but only mark it haphazardly.

My daughter visits the mammals, as does the runt. When she approaches them, they bow their heads and lift dark shining stones in front of their faces. I have seen her raise her tail and perk her ears as though she, not I, were the pups' mother. Even though I have pinned her and taken her by the neck, she returns to their site and struts around their nests.

The runt consorts even more. When he should be out chasing hares, he is off among their nests begging morsels and tidbits. He plays tug-of-war with the burlier one with the shaggy brown fur about his face and head. When I crested the hill recently, they were fighting over a narrow red tuft of fur the length of two foxes. The mammal tugged, and the runt snarled, lowered his hindquarters, and yanked back. But it is only a game. There is no real competition, and the runt learns nothing of life's toughness from it. The mammal, who could have torn the tuft from the runt at any moment, was merely playing. He hung on, tugged repeatedly but never as hard as he could, tossed back his tangled mane, and loosed that strange repetitive bark of his. Afterward, I did not even pin and punish the runt. Life will teach him that begging and playing will never sustain him.

△

Darkness encroaches—the time of orange half-light. Ice herds the fjords, trapping the shrunken bergs. Gusts swipe the hills and cut the valleys. The jaegers and terns have flown. The musk oxen have moved farther afield, seeking higher ground that will remain windswept during even the long night's fiercest snowstorms. We have no choice but to trek after them, though the high edges of our world are severe and the nomadic life is even more uncertain.

We have not had a kill here in more than half a moon. My pups and I are already hungry, and the hard times have not yet begun. Not all of us will survive the coming darkness. Never have all of my pups made it through. I will return to this den when light emerges again, but neither all of the adults in my family nor all of my pups will. It is a natural part of life that no mother ever quite gets used to.

The up-mammals are growing restless. They bumble about their nests and bustle after my mate whenever he so much as lifts his leg to re-mark a stone or drinks from the creek crackling with ice. It is as though the up-mammals must complete their life cycle while it is still light. As though they will vanish with the sun. As though they are afraid of the coming dark. As well they should be.

The up-mammals may have colorful coats, but they have no thick undercoat like ours. I know. I have seen them shed their coats and run howling into the fjord. Their skin looks like a mother's chest after untold pups have suckled for too many moons. And like our pups, the up-mammals know nothing of wind so sharp that you must curl into yourself and cover your nose with your tail to prevent your breath from freezing inside you. They have lost their tails—not so much as a bear's nub. And, with their unlimited droppings from the mammoth black bird, they also know nothing of the hunger that comes from a full moon without a kill...the withering hunger from which siblings and offspring sometimes never wake.

△

We all mill around my porch, all of us, even my pups who must come to understand this if they are to thrive. Clouds streak the sky, and snowflakes whip. Scents jumble. My brother grovels, as he always has, before my mate. He crouches low, his tail tucked under, his neck extended, his ears flattened, and his eyes on the stones dusted with snow. A soft, rhythmic whining escapes his closed mouth.

It has already been decided, and his obsequiousness will

do him no good. Staring him down, I open my mouth and bare my canines. He wags his tail at the ground and whimpers to my mate, who stands tall, his tail raised and his ears erect. My son and my daughter stand behind my mate, but my pups, not yet fully aware of what is occurring, continue to nip at each other.

All of us adults have known that one of us must go before times become too lean. Ordinarily, my son, as the yearling, would be the first to desist, but he is bigger and stronger and more useful to me and my family. True, my brother's wound has mostly healed, but his gait has shortened and his step has slowed. His value, never great, has diminished. His contributions have always been minimal, his utter submissiveness keeping him part of the family after my mother's exile when he himself was a yearling.

I snarl at him until he turns toward me, his ears still pressed back against his skull. He cannot look me in the eye. My pups stop their snipping. He turns his bowed head toward my mate, whose hair is rising. My mate barks at him until my brother's whimper chokes. My son and daughter snarl him around, but he turns full circle until even my pups join us. Neck still extended and coat sleeked down, he looks into my eyes for a moment before turning tail. He trudges slowly to the path leading down to the fjord. As he fades into swirling snow, he does not look back—and I do not howl. I have just seen in his eyes the dull, aching death of dispersal.

△

I howl a second time, but the runt still does not respond. As my family files from my porch into the gusts of snow, I allow my mate to lead this first leg of our journey. I come after him, my daughter follows on my tail, and my son on hers. My three pups trot along behind. The runt should be holding up the rear, but he has wandered off again at the wrong time. He is probably scavenging like a fox from the up-mammals who are tearing apart their nests. They will likely attempt to follow us, but they are too ungainly to keep up. And, they will never survive in the bleak and wind-whipped highlands.

The runt should know better than to ignore my howl. The world will not forgive him. The path we traverse is slick with new snow, but my footing is sure. My hip has almost healed, and, though I still have pain and sometimes stiffness, especially when striding downhill, it is nothing I let the others notice. The runt will catch up—or he will not. Like my brother, he has always been odd, never really fitting in with my family. And his incessant consorting with the mammals has only exacerbated his strangeness. He will race to catch us, but he is too immature. He lacks stamina as well as sense. He should have known by now that if he does not come when I call, he will be lost.

△

As we crest the second ridge, the mammoth black bird's

distant thunder rises behind us. It rolls steadily toward us through brisk wind and dim light. My mate glances over his shoulder and growls but doesn't lose a step. I halt momentarily, allowing my daughter and son and pups to pass into safety between my mate and me. They file by, heads lowered and ears pinned. I raise my head but do not howl at the din echoing around the valley. We climb a third ridge strewn with weather-sheered boulders bigger than oxen. Ahead, a squall lowers and skids toward us, swallowing the next ridge and blowing icy flakes that sting my nostrils.

The great dark beast roars down through the clouds and swoops over us. Though the bird has never harmed any of us, my pups still cower beneath its noise, their damp fur rising in clumps. The beast circles twice, whipping sounds and scents into a frenzy, and then arcs suddenly back into the clouds. Its roar recedes, but only some, and heads toward my den and the valley where the mammals it delivered two moons ago are crushing their nests. My family mills about as though an electrical storm has just struck—until finally I bark them back into line and get them on the move.

I take the lead from my mate who is growling at everything and nothing. The great beast's roar heightens and then abruptly ceases. The runt is lost. Gone for good. He has not howled, not even once, and his legs won't carry him fast enough now to catch us. The approaching squall line will bewilder him if the great bird's thunder hasn't already. Ice crusts my muzzle, and at the ridge's apex the wind slaps my face. The runt has missed his call and must wander alone toward his final breath.

△

My family is exhausted. For days we have marched long, slept little, and eaten nothing but snow. Hunger gnaws now, a deep void formed by our going much of a moon without a kill. My pups are almost as large as me, and their appetites are greater than mine. Though we have confronted herds of musk oxen, each formed its tight flank-to-flank defense—and we had to move on. Now, I follow a set of hoof tracks through the trampled snow, the scant scent keeping me going.

The short, cold, gray day is marked by the usual squalls, which seldom drop significant snow, and wind that burns my pups' eyes. As I lead my family toward yet another wind-scoured ridge, I catch, only for a moment, a stronger smell—musk like that of the dumb ox that blundered onto my front porch. The herd is still out of sight, but one ox must have fallen behind. I can't yet see him either, but I sniff his anger and frustration. The oxen have been rutting for weeks now, the males battling for breeding privileges. Some bulls stupidly spend all of their time defending their females rather than eating. Sometimes losers, having gone lame or otherwise been badly hurt, are left behind.

His nostrils twitching, my mate notes the scent, too. And

then the rest of the family does as well. I stare my pups silent for we *need* this kill, and they would bound down unchecked into the next valley as they did when the runt crashed into the mammals' nest. We must get whatever awaits us to flee rather than stand and fight—and surprise is critical. We spread like a flock forming in sky, my mate and adult daughter angling away from me and my yearling son and my pups.

My mate and I pause at the ridgeline, and there below us, only half a mile away, an old bull trods alone through the snow. He is neither lame nor injured, but his shoulders stoop and his head swings heavily. Without harem or herd, he trudges wearily toward his end. The valley is steep and narrow, almost a gorge. The stinging wind favors us, too, carrying his scent to us and blowing ours away from him. His hooves sink through snow with every step, and my paws barely break the crust.

△

We approach the ox's flanks quietly, my pups obediently behind me. Given our hunger and fatigue, our attack must be short and swift. Only my mate and I could sustain a prolonged chase. When my male pup's forelegs crack the snow, the ox raises his head and bellows. As one, we bound toward him. He is slow to speed, as though his bulk can't find the pace it once did. Trying to climb the slope, he slips, smashing his horns into the snow. Bellowing again, he veers back down.

My mate seizes the ox's right flank, and I race toward the

savagely shaking head. But my daughter is already there. As I am about to leap, she clamps the beast's nose. Somehow, his slashing horns miss her chest. My yearling son snaps at the beast's left flank, and my three pups dash about his rear, not quite sure where to attack. The beast swings my daughter furiously, but she holds fast.

I go for the throat. Hitting hard and deep under the shaggy chin, I force my whole being into my jaws. The throat cracks between my canines, and blood surges into my mouth. He stops, tries one more desperate time to throw my daughter and me off, and then turns circles. I tighten, crushing his throat. His hooves stomp the snow as his circles slow. My pups have his rump and left hind leg. The beast stumbles; blood bubbles into my mouth. My muzzle steams with his blood and breath.

When he topples, my daughter and I are thrown together. She leaps free, but I only bite harder. He flails, though he is already lost. His head jerks in paroxysms. I squirm from beneath his neck, ground my feet, and rip. Before his shuddering stops, my family is tearing at him. Though my mate and I will have the rich entrails, the beast's best, no one will wait to eat. My son and pups are already yanking at the wounds in the flanks before my mate has finished pulling open the belly. Steam swirls around his head and mine. My daughter is here, too, and though I snap at her, she only moves around my mate and buries her muzzle in the heat next to him.

△

Stars turn and northern light pulses through the relentless night. Meteors shower. The wind screams among the old ox's bones, and we are hungry again. We have stripped every morsel from the carcass and sucked the frozen marrow, but now the seven of us are moving on. It is that or starve in this gorge. We have little time. I can see death in my pups' vacant eyes, feel it in my own shrunken entrails, taste it in the snow that never sates, touch it in the ribs beneath my pups' heavy winter coats, and smell it in the gelid air devoid of every scent but that of ice.

We set out together, but the snow is deep and the trekking is tough. We should have gone sooner, but my mate insisted on gleaning all the marrow. Each step depletes my energy now, and my pups struggle more. The thick fur on their haunches and beneath their bellies cakes with snow, and their gait becomes plodding. Despite my growling, they have with their childish games burned too much of their portions of the ox. And now, the wind and cold are teaching them that they should have conserved their strength. Now, winter is inexorable.

Time passes differently here than in the light of summer. Cold slows and stiffens us. We stop more often, curl more closely together to sleep, and wrap our tails more tightly across our noses. Winter is longer, of course, but it feels longer, too. The energy required to stay alive escalates as our food supply diminishes. My strength wanes with time, and my pups falter. The musk oxen grow weak, too, but they are not yet vulnerable. Pursuing the wrong kill might well kill us.

△

My male pup is missing. After a bitter march without nourishment, we nested in a semicircle beneath a cold stone moon. Sleep nipped at me while my enervated female pups straggled in. When he did not arrive, I waited, howled, and waited more. I tried to rouse my mate and son and daughter, but they won't expend their last energy to find him.

I stand and howl at the fixed star around which all the others turn. But it is silent—like the moon. Only the wind answers, and it wails. I lower my head, hunch down, and wait. The darkness offers nothing. My family's breathing is low—close, but so distant it might as well be beyond this world.

I set out alone. The tracks are already windblown, and the scents barely linger. My nostrils freeze, but I still follow all of our scents but his back into the deep blackness. He must be coming. My offspring would never simply give up. Nor can he have gone lost like the runt. He has always heeded my howl. I stop and raise my voice to the infinite silence beyond the wind. Northern light licks the world, but only the wind yowls back.

Finally, I cross his scent. Suddenly, he is here—but not here. The sky is clear, but the wind is whipping old snow about, piling and re-piling it in mounds. It is, though it seems impossible, even colder in this spot. My tail curls under me, but I perk my nose. I turn about, circle, and then widen my circle until I come upon the rock that isn't a rock.

I scrape the snow, pawing...pawing...pawing. He doesn't help. He doesn't even move. Beneath, he is curled—but stiff and cold. His tail is frozen to his nose. I lick his frosted eyes and his brittle ears that haven't heard my howl.

I circle twice more, brushing snow. I growl orders; I even whine. But he won't awaken. I stand full, lift my head, and howl at the expanse of snow and darkness and this world that never relents. I howl at the fixed star, mute as always. I howl to my family who will not come. They know from my voice, my cadence, that there is nothing they can do here. And yet I go on howling, my voice hollow without my family's response, without the inherent disharmony that has marked our songs through time and throughout the world.

But I cannot leave my pup, not now, not yet. I can't *not* be here. I circle, sniffing for what is no longer here. I snip and bite and tug. And then I curl about him, though he holds no warmth. I breathe on him, but he has no breath to return. I might as well be curled around the desiccated bones of an ox.

△

Time. The snow blowing over us holds in my warmth but does nothing for my pup. My family howls me to them, but I cannot move on. Flakes tumble and pile. The wind banks the mound of snow we are becoming. The gnawing emptiness in my stomach is nothing compared to the deeper void.

And time again: turning stars and streaking meteors and swirling snow and my heart beating against ice. The air freezes in my nose, and cold seeps beneath my undercoat. The call of my family recedes. They have encountered something, but their fading howls barely reach me. So far away now. Toward the periphery of this world. And my world shrinks to this hump of snow and this frozen pup. I must leave but can't yet go. I sleep and wake and sleep.

And time turns again until there's sniffing that's not mine. And pawing, like mine but not. The scent...not my mate's... mine and not mine. My adult daughter is here, her warm breath on my nostrils. She has returned with the wider world, the world beyond this heap. I lift my head and blink my crusted eyes as she scrapes snow from my back. I rise, too stiff to walk, too stiff at first even to stretch. Finally, I shake off snow and death as though they were water.

She circles, steps away, and coughs, regurgitating meat into the snow. My hunger seizes me as steam rises from her offering. With that aroma, my hunger becomes everything. I gulp her gift, not even chewing, sucking snow with the warm meat. And then I lick the ground around the spot until it is ice.

The snow is already covering my pup again.

△

The kill is almost stripped by the time my daughter and I reach the site. My sated mate does not rise to greet me. My son is more dutiful, pressing ears and bending legs, and my two female pups sniff and whine as they should. My daughter ambles over by my mate who rests near the carcass, a pregnant female.

Because all of the succulent parts have already been taken, I tear at the remaining muscle so that I will get at least some of my share. This kill may well save us. We are always weaker toward winter's end, but so are the musk oxen, who have to scrape through ever deeper snow for even less fodder. This long winter's storms have impeded the herds even more. The likelihood of stragglers will grow when light begins to gather. That has not yet happened, of course, but this kill gets us closer to the moment in which the balance shifts.

As I rip meat off the right hind leg, I find the evidence—a fracture in the femur. No wonder my family took her even without me. Whether she broke her leg during their rutting or later climbing over ice, she was lame. Her infirmity might well prove our salvation. It is possible, though not yet likely, that we will all make it to light and the glacier's next calving. I chew and swallow more sinew so that I, at least, will make it. I will.

△

My daughter prances before my mate as though she, not I,

were the one. She grooms him, too, nipping at the fur along his back. Though he shows no interest, he doesn't shun her as he should. I have snapped at her, but she persists. She tried this last year as well, but my growling then was enough to drive her off. Now, she goes on with her blatant nuzzling. Soon, when I have regained my strength, I will have to teach her a serious lesson.

At four years old, she is physically ready to mate. After all, she went through a full psuedopregnancy last year—and I even allowed her, at times, to nurse my pups. But she is not yet ready to be a mother. She does not know the world well enough. My mate retains interest only in me, of course—and, anyway, she must wait. Her time will come, but not this year. I will permit her to mate when I am ready.

△

Winter drags on; the wind blows from the stars without ceasing. Snow piles more than at any other time of my life. My daughter leads us toward a ridge, cutting the trail through snow to our chests. My pups struggle but cannot keep up. Often, they have to bound through the drifts even though we adults tramp ahead of them. Though they are almost my size, they can't quite manage yet. They remain bound by birth, of course, a sisterhood that half sustains them and half buries them. One does not go on without the other, and, increasingly, they straggle. Each squanders energy that would be better used for her own survival. And both sap my energy.

We have broken off a long and useless confrontation with a herd of seventeen beasts. Foraging through snow this deep has weakened them but also made them even more desperate than we are. I was finally forced to lead us away from their impenetrable phalanx. With so many of them—all emaciated but otherwise healthy—and so few of us, we stood no chance. And now, at least, the scent of another herd is in the air.

My mate took point for a time, but my son seems more interested in nipping after my daughter than in cutting trails for the family. My strength has, for the most part, returned, but I'm still often too fatigued to lead. In any case, I will let my daughter continue with her arduous work. It is good for her—and may tire her enough that she will not harass my mate.

When, near the top of the ridge, she intercepts a musk oxen trail, she stops, stoops, and sniffs. My son and mate join her, and then I, having slowed to stay in touch with my pups, catch up. My mate paws and snorts. The scent of blood lingers in the snow. Some beast that passed this way was already bleeding. The herd has traversed the valley below, but a dark stain lies still in the snow halfway up the next rise. The smell of blood has not gone stale.

$$\triangle$$

As we follow the scent down, something barely perceptible moves near the blotch in the snow. Not one thing, but five swarming like vermin over the immobile ox. And then in the air, there it is: the stench of fox. A band of foxes in their white winter coats has beaten us. The cowards could not have hunted the ox, so it must have already bled out.

My mate and daughter run ahead, kicking snow. My son and I follow on their heels. The foxes are so intent on their scavenging that, even though we have to cross a quarter mile of snow, they fail to react quickly enough. As my mate seizes the largest by the neck, the others bolt. My daughter tears at the flank of another. The three others scatter with the wind. My son hesitates and then gives chase. I take the neck of the one struggling to free itself from my daughter. I clench through muscle until bone cracks and blood runs hot.

My daughter lets the flank go and gallops after my son. My heart pounds, and, though I am panting, I turn with dangling fox toward my mate. The tail and flanks of his fox brush an arc through the drift when he faces me. Our eyes meet. We each shake the limp foxes. In this long dark winter, blood spots the snow black below each of our muzzles.

The ox carcass is a mother who miscarried. The foxes have ripped apart her fetus but have not yet taken much of her. She is stiff but not yet frozen through. Her empty eyes are open wide, and her head is pulled back as though her last act was to huff at the snow and stars. My mate and I toss away the foxes and turn to the task. My daughter and son return without more kills; my wayworn pups finally arrive. And my family, all of us together, set to the stricken ox.

△

Now that we adults, at least, will likely survive the winter, my daughter is growing too frisky. When we have finished a trek, she brushes up against my mate as though it were the most natural thing in the world. She sleeps nearer to him each time we rest. She won't stop prancing and wheedling. She even rolls on her back before him. My hormones are rising, too, but not as sharply as in past years. And nothing like hers. I have to snap at her every time she nuzzles him— and it grows old.

And, my mate...my mate has begun to bow to her almost as often as to me. Whenever she howls about anything, he too raises his voice to the pulsing light and circling moon. He tosses and tips his head as though she and I are *both* his. They have walked pressed together even more than he and I have. And once—only once—he laid his legs over her shoulders. I had to snarl her far into darkness.

When she returned, she kept her distance—but only for a time before the touching of noses and the incessant grooming began again. He is *my* mate; he would not even be part of this family had *I* not chosen him. When he entered my world toward night three years ago, my former mate, my daughter's father, had been gored in the thigh, hamstrung so badly that he could barely walk much less run. Though he still lived, he could no longer hunt. The wound was not healing, and there was no chance he would survive winter.

My current mate, who had, just like this summer's intruder, come in alone from the other side of the glacier, brought strength and exceptional speed and a knack for the chase. I welcomed him then, and during our first prolonged hunt, we took a calf and its mother both. My family, including my wounded old mate and my daughter, then a yearling, ate fully for the first time in a moon.

When his injuries took my old mate during those first fierce storms of that long night, my hunter and I slept close. My pups perished as well in that frigid darkness; only I and my hunter and my daughter and my brother came through. And then we went to my den beneath the outcropping to prepare for my new pups.

△

Light sniffs the horizon for a moment—only an ephemeral glimmer, but light nonetheless. We go hungry again and my energy ebbs, but the coming of light is still the coming of light. Though snow still drifts, the wind occasionally slackens.

My pups continue to waste. On the way up the last ridge, they foundered for so long among the icy boulders that I had to descend and then growl them to the top. They have eaten enough to survive, but the depth of the snow and the duration of the dark wind have worn them to the scrawniness of foxes. Now in this first flicker of light, I circle my family yet again to wait for them. My daughter capers before my mate, my son pesters her with sniffs and nudges, and my mate snarls him away. They will all await me, of course, but no longer with the pressed ears and bent legs I deserve.

I return through the valley we have just traversed, but my pups are far behind. My scent is clear, as is my daughter's and the males', but I don't catch the pups' until I have gone more than a mile. They lie below the wind among a heap of boulders. The elder is curled around the younger. They are neither stiff nor cold like their brother, but their eyes are flat in the starlight. Their breathing is quick and shallow—not restful at all. The younger pants and trembles as she gapes at me.

Though I growl, no light rises in either pup's eyes. The elder begins to stand but only lowers herself back when her sister shivers more deeply. Tremors pass through the younger, and so I nuzzle her, licking her mouth. I brush her head and neck with my nose. I tug at her scruff and nudge her gently from her shoulder to her hip.

But she is already lost. All three of us know she does not have long. Like a newborn, she is unable to regulate herself; heat is passing from her with each tremor. The elder curls more tightly around her. Though there is nothing to be done at this point, she wraps her tail across her sister's nose.

I howl at the flickering northern light. I howl at my family nesting on the other side of the valley. I howl at the darkness and cold that are stealing my daughter. I howl at the world which does not care, has never cared, and will never care. I howl beyond this world to my mother and to hers and to the others, all gone. All gone. And yet I go on yowling until I cannot catch my breath.

I lower my head, nuzzle my pup one last time, and growl at her elder sister, who raises her head and turns to me. There is something in her eyes now, a faint, distant light. My growl becomes fierce, but that dim light draws no closer to me. We, she and I, must return to my family, but she is immutable. I nip her scruff, and she snaps back at me without fire. I snarl. The light doesn't flare. Though I bare teeth and raise ears, she only lays her head on her younger sister's neck.

I howl once more—and turn away. I take ten paces before looking back. My younger pup twists her head to me, forlorn, but the elder deliberately refuses to look at me. Like the others before her, she will catch up with me. Or she will not.

My family waits for me at the other end of the valley.

△

A lonely light scratches the horizon. Though the chill no longer seeps, weariness floods. Another fresh kill fills my stomach but does nothing for the greater emptiness. My eldest pup has gone silent. For a time, I heard her howls trailing us, and I went on howling her to me. But during the last storm, a gale with biting winds and nose-stinging snow, she went quiet, and I have heard nothing since. The sky is a vast void spattered with stars.

So now I lead my mate and my daughter and my son away from the bones of the old ox we cornered against the rocks. Though he was alone and hobbled, he turned his hindquarters to the stone and faced us, hooves flailing and horns slashing to the end. My son suffered a gash in his right shoulder, and my left hip is damaged again from a fall I took while barely dodging those lethal horns. My mate and daughter came through the skirmish unscathed.

Twice in the last three years all of my pups have perished. I now have only this daughter and son to show for my seven years of labor and pain and care. Other offspring from my former mate have survived and dispersed, of course, and occasionally I have heard a distant howl that I recognize. But they are all loners or members of other families and reside far from me. I no longer even know which of them still lives.

Both my son and daughter are fine physical specimens, but neither remains fully respectful. He isn't yet mature enough to be a father, but that doesn't stop him from shadowing my daughter and snuggling her whenever she lets her guard down. She herself has become almost uncontrollable. She has taken to leaking blood into her urine. Though I have not yet begun to spot the snow, she marks it regularly. And my mate is covering her marks more often than mine. She has even enticed him to sniff her genitals. In truth, his nudging and licking do little for me. His attention and his half-hearted shows of affection irritate me as much as they amuse me. I've had to click my jaws at him repeatedly. In due time, I will again give him enough of my attention. But now I hear only the voices of those I have lost.

△

I thrust to tear out my daughter's throat, but she leaps aside—and I snatch only the coarse hair of her neck. She circles to her right, angling for my injured left flank. I stare, and she wrinkles her nose. When I bare my teeth, she snarls back. I raise my tail higher and wag it harder. My mate stands at a distance, his ears perked and his eyes bright. My son paces behind him, his head nodding.

The far horizon may be glimmering, but darkness permeates my heart. She would not stop yanking at my mate's coat, presenting her rear to his nose, and even moving her tail to the side to expose herself. She wouldn't desist no matter how ferociously I growled. Though I nipped her scruff, she did not turn tail. I had no choice but to attack her.

And now it has come to this confrontation, just as it did with my mother and me. When it was my time to mate, I was forced to drive her, lame and bleeding, from the family. But I will never myself be driven. It is not my daughter's time—not now and not with *my* mate. She must know this, and yet she circles.

I twist and turn, keeping my flank from her. Yelping, she closes. My heart thunders as I pull my hip back. Too fast, she seizes my flank. Pain flashes. She could rip me into frailty in this instant, but she hesitates. I strike back, tearing half her ear off. She lets go and steps away, but whimpers for only a moment. My hip burns from her bite. Blood stains her coat along her neck. I shake my head and spit the piece of her ear.

As she circles, she slowly distances herself. Though I have clearly won, she is not retreating, whining, into the dark. Her tail and her good ear remain raised. I wag my tail and snarl. She continues to back off, but she neither bows nor lowers her tail. When I take a step toward her, ready to leap, my left hind leg buckles. Only for a moment. I arch my neck and wrinkle my nose. She half turns and trots away—but not far enough and definitely not forever. The blood on my flank is already clotting in the cold wind. Though my son rushes after her, it will do him no good. Eyes still gleaming, my mate sniffs the wind.

△

My mate and daughter are locked! Lying in the snow, the deed done, they have already swiveled and settled back to back. Still bound to each other, they are hunkered down just beyond a frigid hummock not far from where I was napping. Their shared heat has melted them a shallow nest. My mate's head is turned away, but my daughter gazes up at me sated and, despite her ruined ear, content.

I lunge at her. She leaps up, breaking their bind and throwing him off. He yelps painfully and turns howling in a circle. She is fast but not quite fast enough, and I catch her between her shoulder and neck. She rips free but not before I have torn muscle and tasted blood. Our eyes meet for an instant—there is no respect there, but no longer contentment either—and then she flees. As she races headlong away, her tail jounces and her feet kick up snow. My mate still howls in pain.

I give chase, but, because my injured hip slows me, I can only stay on her tail for a few moments. I do not, though, stop following until she is far into the darkness. Finally I pause, panting hard, her blood no longer hot on my tongue and teeth. She continues retreating, diminishing with each step. This time, she will not return. She knows I will never allow it, not under any circumstances. But I realize that, unfortunately, she has already gotten exactly what she wanted.

△

My long hunting trip with my mate has proven fruitless—and draining. We stalked seven herds of musk oxen, but none was vulnerable. Though some of the individuals were feeble, they were protected by their herds. My wounded hip has slowed me only a little, but enough to keep me from out-flanking the beasts and causing stampedes. And, with only the two of us, frontal attacks were impossible.

I have not seen my daughter since I had to chase her into darkness. The wound I inflicted on her was certainly not fatal, but she has not so much as howled, which is exactly how it should be. I left my son to fend for himself so that I could be alone with my mate. My son will go hungry, but he will not starve.

Although no direct light yet washes across our world, the peripheral glittering spreads. My heat has passed—but not before I had my mate mount me. He has been dutiful in all respects, but the nuzzling and nipping of past years has been negligible. He licks my muzzle in greeting but barely grooms me. And though he still sleeps close to me and we have at times while traveling brushed against one another, neither of us prances or cavorts. But his inattentiveness doesn't matter to me as long as he will provide for my pups.

△

When we finally make another kill, a hobbling elder who meandered behind his herd, my hunger is appeased. I allow my son to feed because he helped some in the hunt, but my daughter remains estranged. Though I have intermittently caught her scent, especially near our recent caches, she has not approached me. She has been reduced to pilfering like a fox, and no one survives long doing that.

It is not anywhere near time for me to den, but I still find myself being drawn back to the outcropping where I was born.

I can't feel any life within me yet, but I know it must be there just as it has been in other years. My pups will rise with the sun. I will bear them, and they will seek me in each moment. I will give them breath and heat and milk. I will nudge them into light, and they will flourish, becoming adept and always remaining filial.

△

I howl at the gibbous moon. Feeling an even deeper need to return to the cave of my birth, I plead to the great stone light. My mate hears at a distance, but he doesn't immediately join me. He insists on waiting for the musk oxen to move back in his direction, which they will—but not soon enough for me. He procrastinates with hunts that eat time but provide nothing new to eat. For long stretches, he goes off, sometimes with my son but more often alone.

My mate finally catches up to me along the frozen stream I am following toward my den. The trekking has been exhausting, breaking my own trail constantly through the drifts. The wind blows steadily in my face. I ache—my hip that's been both injured and wounded, but also my chest and back so much so that my breath is never completely free. I'm always a little tired, and sometimes simply putting one foot in front of the other is difficult. I keep waiting to feel life within me.

My mate brushes me as he goes by and then leads through the snow so that my path is easier. My step picks up only for a moment, and soon he glances over his shoulder and adjusts his pace to mine. When we finally stop, I am weary to my bones. I lap some snow and curl up, tail across nose. I couldn't cover his mark if I wanted to.

My mate howls to our son who, though I haven't picked up his scent, must be coming after us. He paces back and forth for a time and then settles with his back against mine. His warmth helps but is not enough. Heat leaches from me. I am not yet shivering, but I can't quite hold my heat as well as I always have.

Though I have not eaten in half a moon, I'm not really hungry. I am certain, however, that I will make it to my den without having to hunt. I need to reside there far more than I need food or anything else. I will return, and my mate will accompany me all the way. I will prepare my den as always. My pups will feed from my teats, scrabble around my porch, and yelp at the moon for me.

△

My step falters toward the crest of the ridge. My breathing is heavy, and my gait is not as lithe as it should be. I still look fine—my teeth are strong, and my coat is shiny—but I don't feel good. My mouth and nose are dry. My heart does not beat regularly in every moment. It changes pace far more often than I do. Sometimes it rushes ahead of me even when I am not climbing. I'm not able to slow it, but then it slows without me until all I want to do is close my eyes.

At times, my muscles twitch, and at others they cramp. I feel cold even when I'm moving. I create heat well enough, of course, but I seem to lose it despite my fine coat. Light brushes the horizon for short intervals, but the sun still has not appeared. I find no warmth here at all—and no life burgeoning within me.

When my mate pauses along the ridge, I stop as well. Stars flicker in the depths of sky. A waning moon is rising. Though there have been no new snowfalls on my journey, ice crystals sting my eyes. I want to scratch a nest out of the wind, but this is no place to rest.

My mate's call is strong and clear. The wind carries it behind us across the valley and out toward the peaks so that his deep voice reverberates through the world. I circle and sniff, trying to catch my breath. My son, distant but not out of range, returns the call. He is well behind us but heading toward my den as well.

When there is a second, higher call, I freeze. The hair of my scruff lifts in the wind. Raising my tail and growling, I turn toward my mate. *She* is following, too. She knows she is unwelcome, but she accompanies my son anyway. My mate's head is turned away as though he has just caught the musky scent of a herd. My snarling is disregarded. Ignored! If she comes too close, it will be the last thing she ever does. He must know that, but without looking back he begins to descend among the rocks.

I start to shiver. We are too close to my den not to follow. Another two ridges and I will see my fjord and my outcropping. The stones of my porch and the dark mouth of my cave will welcome me. I will rest in my den's deeper darkness out of wind and worry.

△

Snow has blown across the mouth of my cave. I've never returned this early—more than a moon before the equinox—but it is necessary this year. As my mate climbs my outcropping to announce our arrival, I scratch the crusty snow away from the opening. I am spent, the last leg of the journey having taken just about everything out of me. Each time I paused to eat snow I had diarrhea. Even now, I cramp; my breath is heavy and uneven.

I wriggle through the hole into the darkness. Shaking, I descend, turn, and climb into my den. Though it is all familiar, it's not right. The scent of life is missing. No redolent aroma tells of squirming pups or mother's milk or high-pitched yelping. The air provides no hint of vitality at all. I curl, quivering, into myself. Outside, my mate howls to the others, his voice resounding. Inside, there is only fathomless darkness and cold.

△

My vomit steams on the snow by my porch. I gag and retch the rest of the cached meat my mate brought me. Shivering beneath gusts of wind that swoop from the stars, I stagger back away. My coat is covered with the urine and excrement I can no longer control. My ribs ache with each breath I take, and a sharper pain claws at the left side of my chest.

When my mate lowers his head to take the meat I cannot eat, I snap at him. He snarls back, and I raise my ears. He'll just give the meat to *her*. Though I have not seen her, I have smelled her. She is nearby—far too near.

Still teetering, I pace my porch, mustering my strength for a final confrontation. But I can barely even raise my head to growl again at my mate, who has gobbled all the meat. Ears lowered and head tilted almost deferentially, he steps toward me. I bare my teeth. Though my snarl is cut off, like a cough, he backs away.

△

The tight darkness of my den provides refuge from the wind, but I can't stop shivering. I continue to retch even though there is nothing, not even bile, left in my stomach. The quavering slows but also deepens. I wobble to my feet and rock against the rock. The walls pulse like northern lights. Meteors shower behind my eyes. My muscles seize, and my breath falters. I alternately grit my teeth and gasp. My bowels repeatedly cramp and release.

I hear howling outside, my mate's voice rising and falling in the sweeping wind. I can only cough back. Other voices join his, a chorus that fails to be unharmonious. My son's voice swells, but so, too, does my daughter's—an intrusive, infuriating yowl. I paw at the frozen sand and dig my face into it until I collapse. Pain jerks me to my feet again too soon. Too soon.

Voices echo about me, converging through time and space. Every pup I ever bore chants, as do all of my relatives, close and distant, and their pups. My old mate, my banished brother, and the father I knew for only one bright summer unite in song. And then, too, my mother, whom I chased into darkness, and her mother, whom I never knew, and hers, and hers—all sing a deafening, woeful dirge.

All of them crowd so closely into my den that I cannot breathe. I snap and snarl, but they shift and sidestep and reform, stalking me, every one of them, as though I were some doddering ox. All of their voices merge into one—my mother's. She howls within this den and atop this outcropping and throughout this world.

I am a pup again, still blind, scrabbling for first milk, then toddling into dazzling light, and then battling my siblings for the best morsels delivered by my father. I am running down my first hare, cutting sharply, seizing its head, tasting hot blood. I am giving chase to a behemoth, having him turn horns and hooves on my family, and watching my father's chest heaving, spewing blood with each gurgling breath. I am bending under dark wind licking the scruff of my starved sister gone stiff in that first long night.

My mother's voice rises, reverberating through this dank den smeared with my waste. I wheel and snarl and snap, but the din only intensifies. I am seizing the back of my mother's neck, teeth deep, not letting go until her ears flatten, her knees bend, and her voice becomes a hoarse whine. I am nuzzling my first mate, sniffing and being sniffed. I am licking the fluid from my squirming daughter and from the others, all the others, each and every one of my pups.

Now, as the others' voices commingle again with my mother's, I want, more than anything, to feel life within me. Once more. Just one more time. I want to chew through my umbilical cord and eat the sac. I want to smell the richness of birth rather than this moribund stench. I want to feel quick beating and warm breath and hard gums searching for my milk.

But my breath only catches, and my mouth hangs open like a dead fox's. My limbs stiffen as I spasm. I pant and twitch. The world, my world, begins to slip from me. The light behind my eyes fades into that deeper night. The keening, far away, far beyond me now, subsides.

We shall not cease from exploration
And the end of all our exploring
Will be to arrive where we started
And know the place for the first time.

Little Gidding
T.S. ELIOT

Whale Song

I came into this world flukes first. Light broke around me, vast and blue. Stroking me, my mother nudged me toward air. My first breath was tangy, my lungs filling and every cell welling as I breached in those Pacific waters.

My flukes unfolded. Two of my aunts prodded me along. Clumsily, I swam in the swells. I needed my mother's milk as much as that August air, and so I dove beneath her. As she slowed, I took her nipple. Her sweet rich milk streamed down my throat. My aunts and cousins sang to me. All about me, the sea and sky clicked.

＆

This is my song, a hymn of life—my life and yours. My song is at once beautiful and painful. At times a ballad and an anthem. By turns a psalm and a lampoon—as we would expect from life. Not often an idyll, and never a lullaby. Not a dirge either, for I am not submerged in the inevitable losses of our lives. But a chant, a canticle, a litany.

I am, by nature, gentle. Even shy, at least around those outside my family and friends, my clan. And I hope you will remember this because some of what I sing is neither gentle nor bashful. When, at times, my song sounds harsh, it is that so much is at risk—our survival, certainly, and yours, as well. I do know that we are bound, as sure as a harpoon is to its line. So know that even when my words are sharp, when my barbs strike deep, I am, at the far end of the line, a gentle soul.

You have not yet understood or heeded our songs. Perhaps, you never will. But I will do my best to have you hear me before it is too late. Before all of the songs, ours and yours, sink into time's depth and darkness. Listen. My life depends on it. Your life depends on it.

＆

I weighed only a ton when I was born, but now I am enormous. My mother's milk was high in protein and minerals and, yes, fat—and I grew prodigiously. Now, as I approach my sixtieth birthday, I am just under sixty feet long and weigh fifty-nine tons. Indeed, now I *eat* a ton on a good day, and my blubber remains thick. My four-hundred-pound heart pumps five gallons of blood at a beat. Despite my gargantuan size, I am fast. Normally, I travel at four to seven knots; I dive at three. But I can swim at twenty knots when I need to. I'm not bragging. I just need you to know who I am.

My eyes look small because of my bulk, but they are two-and-half inches in diameter. Absolute size controls functioning in eyes—as it does, to a certain extent, in brains. My eyes really are large, and I see well—except, of course, that my huge head causes quite a blind spot. In fact, my head is one-third of my body, about twenty feet and twenty tons: I am the largest of the Toothed Cetaceans. But Blue Baleens are far bigger—the largest animals who have ever lived in this world. So my size is relative, titanic to you but not to a Blue.

☿

I don't really look like anything else in this world. You would, I suspect, think me ugly. And, I suppose I am. My head is squarish—*blockish*, you might say. It contains the largest brain ever as well as vast amounts of spermaceti, the oil for which you slaughtered my ancestors. My blowhole is a slit on the left near the front of my head. My blow is bushy, forward, and skewed to the left.

My eyes bulge a bit. I have no visible ears, but I hear far better in water than you. Sound travels through my inner ears, my jaw, and my spermaceti cavity. I have no hair, as most other mammals do, but my blubber keeps me warm and, because it is lighter than water, buoyant. I can open my jaws ninety degrees. My lower jaw is long and narrow and underslung. My teeth—conical, thick, and heavy—fit into slots in my wide upper jaw, which is toothless. My throat is also wide, broad enough, in fact, for you to pass down it.

My skin is creased, *wrinkled*, unlike the smooth skin of other Cetaceans. In the millions of generations since my forebears returned to the water, my arms evolved into short fins with rounded tips. My back has no dorsal fin, just a hump and a series of knobs running toward my tail. My torso is extremely muscular (I have, after all, to propel fifty-nine tons at speed), and I have no vestigial legs at all. My intestines contain ambergris, for which you also massacred my forefathers. It is nothing more than an intestinal by-product, but you still value it beyond measure.

My broad triangular flukes are horizontal—enough for you to know that I am no fish. The trailing edges of my flukes are pretty well frayed. *Scalloped* by life. I have been around a long time, roved the world, experienced much that living offers us all. I realize that my longevity isn't exceptional for a large-brained mammal, but in these last sixty years the changes in our world have been epochal, even apocalyptic. Of these I will sing.

॰

Whenever one of you has spotted me, you have stalked me. You no longer have murder in your hearts, but you still cannot leave me be. I suppose it is my color. I am large, of course, but not much larger than some of my cousins or, had he lived, my brother. My whiteness gets your attention.

Your stalking, understandably, bothers me. My breath quickens, and I don't sing as much. I spend more time on the surface, and I find myself changing course more often than I would like. It's not just your constant noise, though that confuses all of us. Your presence out here doesn't make sense, given all you should be doing on land at this moment.

This pallor of mine occurs every four generations or so in my family. It is not a curse. No one has shunned me, and mating has been anything but a problem. And yet my hue sets me apart. Always has. But it doesn't change who I am. It just is. My color has never mattered to me or to my family and friends. Why should it?

॰

My spermaceti organ protrudes from my head, making my snout stout. You might think *bloated*, even *engorged*. It appears swollen in large males, and I am an especially large male. It runs from under my blowhole to a crease at the back of my head— in my case, more than sixteen feet, with an air sac fore and aft. All in all, a good sized Pilot Whale could swim inside my head.

Using my spermaceti organ, I can produce sounds in pulses that allow me to echolocate and communicate over long distances. I can, whenever I need to, expand my sensory field for many miles. I can also produce sounds intense enough to stun prey and frighten competitors. And, well, females like my organ—both for its size and the intensity of my clicks and calls, codas and chants. You see, for us, acoustic size matters. I sound even larger than I am, giving me certain advantages in attracting females and daunting other males. Then too, my head provides me, when necessary, with an impressive battering ram.

You have always coveted the oil inside my organ. You first slaughtered my forebears for this fluid I use to navigate and communicate. You could have learned a lot from studying our spermaceti organs, these innate systems that do so much of what you need to understand about navigating and communicating. But instead you massacred us. You demonized us and butchered us, sending us to the edge of extinction, but mostly you misunderstood us. You called us *sperm whales* because this oil, an absolute necessity to us and merely a commodity to you, looked like your sperm.

☿

I dive deep. Deeper and longer than any other animal. The greatest breath-holding diver who has ever lived. Often I dive to more than 3,600 feet for an hour at a time. But I have sounded for twice that long to far more than a mile. Boasting again? I hope not. Just letting you know what it is that I do.

I throw my flukes in the air and plunge vertically. My flukes beat hard, but my heart rate drops as I descend. My lungs are extremely efficient, and my muscles store oxygen well. I dive, as I said, at about three knots. My motto is *Do not rush; do not rest.* If I go too fast, I burn too much oxygen; too slowly, and I burn time. At a depth of 800 feet, my lungs and jointed ribcage collapse. Light diminishes, and I start to click. My echolocation is so sophisticated that I really can *see* in sound as the world around me sinks into darkness.

By the time I reach 1,600 feet, it's absolutely dark. The world is cold. Time alters, slows, then vanishes. I can hear distant sounds—storms and earthquakes and the incessant buzzing of your ships. Sometimes, you emit even more discordant sounds, sonar signals and seismic pulses.

At depth, I hunt for squid and octopus; deep-dwelling sharks are good sport, too. Below 3,200 feet, my lungs are flat, but air in my nasal passages still circulates so that I can reflect sounds and create clicks. I flow, lit in an acoustical world. Like you, I am composed mostly of water. And when I go especially deep, I become water. The world beyond, air and sky and sun and stars, evaporates in the aquatic moment.

And here I meet Architeuthis, the giant squid, my most worthy foe—and my favorite food. Though I am one hundred times heavier than Architeuthis, the outcomes of our battles are never foregone. The greatest invertebrate in the ocean, he is superbly fit for life in the deep, with a large brain and gigantic unblinking eyes that provide him with sharp sight in what appears to be total darkness. His funnel propels him forward and backward; ink from his sac provides a concealing cloud. The ringed suckers on his eight arms and two long tentacles are toothy, and his hooked beak is sharp. Indeed, with him I can never be certain that I will return from the hunt's dark depths.

☿

My life is a cycle, the pace slow. I was in my mother's womb fifteen months. I took milk for three years. I was twenty-nine before I was a father. I have been roving, North and South, East and West for more than fifty years. The ocean, my home, cycles with the tides, the day, the moon, the seasons. Though the current runs north and west around the tip of Alaska, it flows south along the rest of the continent. Near the equator, it heads west toward Asia where it turns again and circles back, forming the mammoth North Pacific Gyre. Even our home, the world itself, cycles through the year and through the ages. My pace within these cycles provides me with time to think. My thoughts cycle, too, between good and evil, comedy and tragedy, hope and despair.

Your thoughts would cycle, as well—if you took the time. But you are too busy. And your busyness, your business, hurtles you toward the apocalypse. There will be flood and fire, strife and starvation, carnage and catastrophe. Your home, our world, will howl.

And yet, and yet my thoughts cycle. Our destruction isn't predestined. At this moment, the light dances on the water, the sparse clouds form runes, and the current whispers to me, even as the melting ice moans and the calving bergs groan. Ice has always sung its own sad song, but it is transmuting now— fast becoming a requiem. Here and in the Southern Ocean.

♂

Life has scarred me from head to flukes. It can't be helped, of course. Life does it to us all. The front and top of my head are thoroughly cross-hatched. Tattooed by the beaks and suckers of Architeuthis. But, in truth, my head is scored as much by the teeth of other Cetaceans.

We males fight. We compete for the right to mate. None of us mates every year, and some of us never become fathers. Our battles are real, not ritualistic. When I was younger, I fought hard, attacked with my whole being. I gnashed my teeth and flailed my flukes. I broke jaws, but I never killed another Cetacean. Never.

Even though I didn't lose a battle for a decade and a half, I only fathered five offspring. Our reproductive rate is lower than that of any other animal. Three of my daughters survived to adulthood, and two are now themselves mothers. One has already lost a baby, an event from which she has never quite recovered. You see, females only bear a child every five or six years. Twins are rare. The young die far too often, and mothers do not easily get over their deaths. My daughter carried her son in her mouth for a week after he died.

☿

The sun is heading south. Fall is here, and I am leaving. It is time. Time to descend from the higher latitudes as I sing to you. Time to return to the Galapagos, to the sea of my birth where this song began for me.

Winter is coming, but even here in the Gulf of Alaska it is not what it once was. Fall arrives a bit later now, and spring earlier. I can feel the difference in the water. It is warmer, perhaps even a full degree. The current is changing, too—not a lot yet but enough so that we who live here can't help but notice the shift. And all life as we know it will turn with the current. I hope you are finally beginning to comprehend how much the currents affect us all. How much the currents influence even your life.

I have put Polaris behind my flukes. I am again pelagic, the seafarer roving one last time. Everything wheels through the night sky around the polestar. The wheeling is beautiful, the night sky cycling as the year does. And our lives. But the North Star, fixed, is guide and constant companion to a solitary wanderer. Though it is immensely distant, it seems close, its light touching my back whenever I breathe. Constancy does that. Gives us the feeling, the illusion, if you will, of closeness. And I understand that even Polaris is slowly shifting, that one night it, too, will wheel, no longer due north, the marker of the geomagnetic pole. But I will be long gone. So may we all. My thoughts are concerned with the current spinning, the changes that have accelerated in my lifetime.

I don't know if I will ever return to this gulf. I will miss the flash of light on the distant ice. I will miss the sun shimmering on the water. I will especially miss the Aurora Borealis, the light wavering in darkness, pulsing to the beat of the world, its song calling out to the stars, to the universe of which we are such a small but significant part. I'm not a fatalist, but this may be my last journey, my last song. The world is changing fast, and I am no longer young enough to ignore what is occurring.

$$\text{\male}$$

I will not, however, miss your presence in this gulf. The changes you wreak are radical. I was here, you must remember, when your wayward tanker spewed your crude oil into our waters. I was just returning in the spring of my forty-second year when the tanker tore out its belly and disgorged 44,000 tons of black sludge. I was able to stay far enough from shore to avoid this spreading black plague, but everyone else, from fish to fowl, was infected. Many small marine mammals, particularly seals and otters, perished. The web of life was altered here—perhaps not permanently, but certainly for my lifetime and yours.

And that Black Death almost two decades ago was relatively small—only 1,500 miles of shoreline were damaged. There have been many worse spills, including ten of 95,000 tons or more and four of more than 200,000 tons. But this plague sticks in my mind because it happened in my home—and the recovery will never fully occur in my life. Ironically, the disaster has only driven more of you here with more of your noise and more of your debris discharged into the gulf. I take it all personally because I live here. But you have to understand that the coming catastrophe will be personal for *all* of us, whoever we are and wherever we live.

⚥

As I said, my brain is enormous, the largest of any animal on earth—of any animal that has *ever* lived. Yes, I know, as I myself admit, I am a leviathan. Your brain is larger relative to your size. It is, what, two-and-a-half percent of your body mass? And mine is far less. But there is at times something to be said for absolute size, don't you think? Absolute size marks intelligence in a way relative size does not. I understand, though, that you may remain stuck on relativistic notions, especially when they benefit you.

Just as your brain has evolved to suit the needs of a mid-sized terrestrial mammal within a complex social group living in a sometimes hostile environment, our brains have evolved to suit us. The oceans aren't often hostile (except, of course, when you have made them so). Our social groups are complex, but the situations we find ourselves in generally are not. We simply don't need some of the tricks of which you are so proud.

Your brain is better with olfactory information, and mine is better with auditory. Your environment requires a strong sense of smell, and mine does not. But directional hearing is critical for me. And echolocation—well, if you really understood it, you would be green as algae with envy. And geomagnetic locating...I won't get into that at all. Too much for you, I'm afraid. So we live with our differences: you find me smelly, and I find you noisy.

But both our brains are good at mental processing. We are both wired for intelligence, especially social intelligence. We each have individual personalities. We can make decisions quickly in complicated situations. We can take care of our families and make friends. We can have fun. We can provide help when necessary, and even sacrifice ourselves for others. We form cultures. We learn and pass on that learning to others.

So please don't make the mistake, the perhaps fatal error, of assuming that because you have a relatively large brain, indeed, a remarkable brain, that others lack intelligence. I have learned a lot in my roving. I dive deep, and I journey to and from the higher latitudes. I *think*—in some ways more clearly than you. And, most importantly for this song, I remember.

☿

Yes, we have cultures. Not a Cetacean culture. Not a Sperm Whale culture. But diverse cultures that we have passed on for generations upon generations. For thousands of generations. Tens of thousands. I'm not going to dive into any nature versus nurture argument here. I'm just not. But you need to understand that our societies are not only different from yours and Orcas' and Blues' but also from each others'.

My clan is spread throughout the Pacific, but our ancestral home is off the Galapagos Islands. Our Diaspora, especially following the massacres of my forefathers' time, is as far-flung as the Indian Ocean and the South Atlantic. And yet we remain culturally distinct. Our language is *ours* alone. No other clan communicates as we do. Our songs are never the same as others' songs. We tend toward greater synchronicity in our dances—even in our dives. We are roundabout, traveling more circuitous routes than other clans do. And yet we also venture closer to land which, fortunately and unfortunately, brings us more often in contact with you.

Though the ranges of our foraging inevitably overlap with those of other clans, we generally remain within our clan. Females, especially, live their whole lives with other females of their clan. Of course, intermingling occurs, particularly among roving males. Sometimes thousands of us, male and female from various clans, find ourselves together. Such moments can be celebratory, even raucous, but we remain cognizant of our distinctions. Some seasons we are more successful at foraging, and other seasons other clans are.

In our entire history, age upon age, no clan has ever *fought* with another clan. Such battles simply make no sense in the long sweep of time. Whatever our differences, we realize that we are present, always here and now, alive, bound together in this world, our home. And that understanding, embedded in each of our cultures because of who we are as beings, supersedes whatever differences exist. Our languages and customs may vary, but our connection to sea and sky, air and water, does not. It couldn't possibly.

♻

We sing and dance. Why? Because it's fun, but also because it brings us together. Sometimes we even learn a little about who we are and what we're all doing here. When I was young, my family and others in my clan convened near the surface most afternoons. We met in the best of times and the worst of times. We swam together, logged and rolled simultaneously, and hung vertically, our buoyancy pure. We danced belly to belly, jaws touching, sometimes clasping. We sang our codas, our patterned songs, as solos, duets, even choruses. We side-fluked, making our sharp turns together, and spyhopped to look at that amazing other world of air and sky. We breached and we lobtailed, both of which are infectious. Invariably, once one of us shook the sky, the whole group went aerial. The more families that gathered, the wilder it got. It was all a cracking good time.

I was something of a lobtailing prodigy. I probably sound like I'm bragging again, but I was. Even at the age of three I could strike my flukes on the sea's surface with the best of them. When lobtailing, you can go vertical or horizontal—or really any angle in between—but I was an on-the-surface-straight-ahead horizontal lobtailing virtuoso. I raised my peduncle and flukes just so, and then smacked the water hard—the Crash and Splash. We all lobtail (the more the merrier, actually), but early on I developed a thwacking good Dorsal Down, the reverse lobtail. I'd gather speed, roll onto my back, dip and rise, and shake down the thunder. I also perfected the Cross-Over, a dozen quick ventrals and dorsals, back and forth for a minute or more with no break until I was exhausted and exhilarated.

Now, on those rare occasions when I am with the females and the young, I still enjoy singing and dancing—belly to belly and jaw to jaw. And I still like the attention that a snapping series of Cross-Overs brings.

♀

I had a gift for lobtailing, but I admit that breaching is the most spectacular aerial move we make. There's nothing quite like launching yourself, hurtling airborne until the world's gravity grabs you and flings you onto the water. A relative calm with a bit of wind helps, but the real key to breaching is the dive. You fluke-up, dive fast and deep, flip, and shoot straight for sky. All out. Top speed. A twist in the air as you fly free provides a nice touch, but whatever you do, you have to give it your all—all in, all the way. The Crash and Splash can be beyond belief. A side-landing is best. Belly breaching tends to be jaw-jarring, and back breaching is tough on the blowhole and the spermaceti organ. Any time of day will do, any time at all, but a moonlight breach is especially gratifying.

Now, though, I rarely breach. Part of it is my size—fifty-nine tons is a lot of mass to hurl at the moon. And part of it is, I suppose, maturity. But part of it, too, may be that abandon, unabashed and unfettered, is harder to come by. I know too much about life and what is happening to the world.

☿

I hope I'm not making my early childhood sound too idyllic. There were wonderful moments, to be sure. Some days and nights really were halcyon, the seasons turning with the currents and the temperature. We meandered the Eastern Pacific, foraging beneath the waves and congregating under the sun and stars. But beneath it all, an undercurrent of peril flowed through my family and my clan. It wasn't just the intermittent storms whose swells made me breach just to breathe—

to breach, in fact, for my life. Or the occasional Orca attack that killed some distant aunt's newborn. Or the presence of sharks on the periphery of the clan waiting for some disaster so they too could strike.

No, the deepest threat was *you*. When I was young, you were still slaughtering upwards of thirty thousand of us a year. My clan survived my first year pretty much intact, but we were decimated my second. You might use words like *pod* or *school*, but when you do you miss the point. I may be a leviathan, but I am no fish. When I was young, I was part of a complex and sophisticated and, yes, *related* society that you massacred. Your huge steel ships slew and flayed us with impunity. And without so much as a thought that you were destroying an ancient and intricate culture.

♂

We heard the Killing Fleet long before the ships loomed on the horizon. The deep roar of the Death Factory bellowed beneath the varying snarls of the Killers. We should have scattered in 360 directions at the first sound, but it is not in us to do so. As I said, we live together in a close, related society. And, so, we died together. We congregated in death.

The Killing Fleet moved inexorably toward us at eighteen knots. Most of us are faster, but outrunning them wasn't a choice because we move at the pace of our slowest member. And it would have proved useless, in any case. We tire, but the Killing Fleet does not. Their incessant din drove coherent thoughts from our minds. Panic raced through the clan.

In my forefathers' time, during the earlier slaughters, fighting back sometimes saved lives. The Killers were smaller, quieter, and less mechanical, the harpoons painful but not immediately lethal. Gnashing valiantly and fluking maniacally made survival possible. My famously white forefather destroyed your Killers, stove even your Death Factories, and sent you to the squids' domain. He survived all of your attacks to live a long life, wearing your bones as a talisman. And he was genuinely heroic. You killed his mates and his children and hunted him, and he avenged those he loved. Those he killed may have been brave, but they were not heroic. They died only so that someone far from danger could be a bit more comfortable.

In the killing fields of my youth, there was no place for heroism, only wanton carnage. Impregnable, utterly free from personal danger, your Killers fired harpoons that pierced our skin and exploded inside us. Blood smeared the sea. You murdered the children first, knowing their bereaved mothers would not leave. Confounded by your clamor and panic-stricken by the slaughter, I clung to my mother's clicking. She and I dove, turned, went deeper, twisted, swam as long as we could, breached for a precious breath, and dove again. We found some distance from the insatiable Killers, but we couldn't escape the cacophony.

Only once was I close enough to watch the spiked jaws of your Death Factory hoisting the victims into air. Close enough to hear the horrific tearing apart of my kin, as though the sky itself was rent. Close enough to see my relatives' entrails dumped from clouds of steam into the sea for the sharks and other scavengers. The infernal grinding rose above the din. And though I have almost no olfactory sense, I smelled those boilers blotting the sky with their unholy steam. The stench lingers in my mind to this day.

My mother and I survived that killing season, just as my white forefather did before us. But, to hear my family tell it, he became bitter in the end. Alone. For him, never a good night or a gentle going. His rage against you fouled him from his scarred blowhole to his tattered flukes. His every song, even his last, remained a battle cry. I am not, as I said, heroic like him—but neither am I bitter. Or at least, I am trying not to be. My song is too important to be one of mere ire or past poison. No, the past is past. It is our future of which I sing.

♉

We survivors went on living together—my mother, my remaining aunts and cousins, and I. My father was, of course, off in the higher latitudes, and my older brother had already left the family to rove with friends. But for the next year, my cousins, male and female, were all around me—not just in the afternoons when we played and sang, breached and rolled, lobtailed and spyhopped—but each and every day and night, drawn closer by loss. We never fought. Fighting only came later, with my friends and other males I didn't know. And that was over mating, which hadn't yet entered my mind.

My mother's voice always sang to me. Even when she dove, foraging for us, her voice carried to me. She provided me with milk the whole time. Though I was eating solid food by the time I turned two, she continued to nurse me—as much for the care as the sustenance. She touched me every day.

All of this ended abruptly for me when my mother's song went silent early in my fourth year. Ironically, it wasn't one of your mammoth ships, your Death Factory and your swift Killers, that murdered her. Tangled in your cable, she drowned.

♉

As my mother breathed before her last dive, the clouds broke. Sun streaked down, raining light around us and firing the water's surface. The storm had raged for three days. Lightning had webbed the sky, and the winds had spun white drifts across the water. Twenty-three of us had followed a deep fissure that cut from the abyssal trench almost to the shore—far farther toward land than we usually ventured, but the foraging had been good. All of us had been disconcerted by the ferocity of the storm, but the sudden light made me think danger had passed with the scudding clouds.

Flukes up, my mother disappeared. I stayed aloft, too

young to dive as deep as she. Five of my young cousins were with me, all staying above our elders as they plummeted. The divers began to click in earnest after ten minutes, their songs spreading as they foraged. My mother headed deeper, as was her custom. Her voice rose to me as always. And she was successful, as she so often was. For forty minutes, I listened to her songs and rolled to watch the streaming light.

Almost out of breath, my mother began to rise. When her song first changed, there was little note of alarm. I may have been slow to react—I don't know because the flow of time had already begun to alter before I understood what was happening. My aunts and older cousins converged as though one of us had stranded. And, I suppose, in a way, my mother had. Her voice became strident. The more she struggled, the more tangled she became in your cable.

Her panic lasted only until she heard my stricken cries. She slowed her clicking as I dove. But I couldn't go deep at all. My breath kept catching in my throat. In my panic, I couldn't stay on the surface long enough to fill my lungs. I knew even then that I wasn't old enough to find her dark depth, and in that moment, helplessness washed over me. My inability to do anything struck me more deeply than any harpoon's point. But I still kept up with my shallow, useless dives. It was all I could do.

When her sisters and cousins reached her, my mother stopped struggling. Her song became softer, the love in her voice telling them—and me—to stay clear. And then as they sang to her, her song went silent. I don't think she was dead yet. She knew that if I reached her, I would die, too. And so she no longer called to me.

I dove on into the night. First my cousins and then my aunts, returning from the depths, stroked me. Voices clicked condolences around me. But I was inconsolable. The voice I needed to hear was mute.

♂

I never looked for my mother's body. It was another year before I was capable of diving to that depth. She would by then have been only bone. I have never known, but I imagined that the deep sea sharks were already swarming before she let go her last breath. It is the way of the sea, the way of life.

Once her song was silent, she was gone. My family sang to me, but the voice I longed to hear was missing. There are no orphans among us, however. An aunt suckled me freely, as though I were her son. The nourishment kept me growing, but it never felt the same. I weaned myself in four months. When my family gathered in the afternoons, I lobtailed harder than ever. But, in truth, there was more anger than joy in the crack of my flukes against water.

I stayed another year within the clan, but early in my fifth year, I left with two older cousins who were heading west on their own. Was I too young? Probably, but I was large for my age and still torn from my family by grief. The Killing

Fleet had brought us survivors together in our horror, but the nature of my mother's death, her disappearance into that dark depth, in some way isolated me. And so I went west, too.

☿

My cousins and I joined half a dozen other young males, but we didn't, at first, venture into the higher latitudes. Orcas and sharks were rare in the open ocean, and I learned to hunt Architeuthis and the lesser squid, earning my first scars out toward the North Pacific Gyre. At that time, your garbage had not yet gathered there.

Tsunamis passed us regularly, but they were no threat either. With my echolocation, I can often hear a distant undersea earthquake or volcanic eruption. The subsequent tsunami travels fast, sometimes at 450 knots, but it isn't dangerous. As the wave approaches, the ocean's level rises a few feet. The tsunami passes in twenty to thirty minutes, and the surface falls gently back to its normal level. If your hearing and echolocation aren't acute, you'd barely notice what's happening. Near shore, tsunamis slow to a mere one hundred knots, but the shape of the shallows can, at times, really focus the wave's energy—and all hell breaks lose against the land.

☿

You loosed all hell of a different sort in the Pacific of my first youthful forays. The islands, Bikini and Enewetak, have exotic names and remote locations. Or, rather, *remote* for terrestrials like you, but not for my friends and me. At the far edge of our range, you detonated your most terrifying Marvels.

The first time, the increasing activity of your ships and airplanes let us know you were up to some mischief, but I was too young and naive to comprehend the extent of the horror—your astonishing knack for destruction. I guess there was no way for any sentient being to really understand what you were doing until you had already done it. How could I have been prepared? How could anyone?

The flash, though distant, inverted the day, reversed the horizon. The cloud rose like hell's own jellyfish. The heat slapped the air, then the water. The earth quaked, the sky erupted, and invisible waves of death poured over all of us living in the area. The drifting clouds and noxious rain came later, more slowly and more sickeningly.

Earthquakes, volcanic eruptions, and tsunamis are all natural events, occurrences in the life of the Earth—part of the planet's cycle. Yes, the seascape is sometimes altered. Some species benefit and others suffer. Your technological destruction is, however, *unnatural*. Your explosions, though small compared to the earth's strongest storms, are not part of any cycle. They rain death and obliterate life. In becoming the Destroyers, you set yourselves apart from the world and above the rest of us who live here.

But why? Why would anyone wreak this havoc upon the

world? Even all of these years later, I can't figure out what possesses you.

♂

Now, I am a loner. My song becomes one of solitude. The oldest and largest of us males have always been solitary. I don't mind it, really. Time alone is good. You can think things through, clear up what is in your mind, make connections among your thoughts, find the currents, the ebb and flow, the cold and the warm, and feel them purl.

After I left my family, I lived another seventeen years with friends, a fraternity of sorts. That's the way our culture works. But our fellowship eventually broke up over mating. That, too, is our way. And now, as I have said, I live alone. I never lived with my father. In fact, I only met him half a dozen times, twice when I was very young and he returned to mate, and four times, by chance, later in my rovings. I really only knew him through his songs. He was not bitter like my white fore-father, but his songs did have a motif, a recurring theme: The life of the mind is a lonely one. The price each of us pays for thought is solitude. He was, I think, right.

But I do still, after all of these years, miss the others. I will at some point in this journey visit the females and the young of my clan. I won't mate, though. I will not bring any more young into this world. But I miss the attention from the females when I mated. I miss the cavorting with friends and family. I miss the interplay, the playfulness. I still need on occasion the company, the companionship, the touch, the feel of others around me. I remain, even in my solitude, irresistibly drawn to others.

Indeed, even to you. For the most part, you no longer massacre us. The Killing Fleets dwindled, eventually eradicating themselves even as they attempted to annihilate us. And then the Killers vanished. There are rumors that they still hunt and hew near the Asian islands, but I haven't myself heard their ominous rumble in decades. Recently, you have, on occasion, even tried to save us.

I don't want to offend you because I need you to continue to listen to my song. But you have to understand that you are still destroying us, *all* of us in this world. Despite all of the Marvels you have created—the artifices and the ships and planes that move you so swiftly through the water and air—you have forgotten so much of what you need to know to live, to keep this planet, *our* home, alive. Your mechanical Marvels become ever bigger and faster, but your life does not become better. Not really.

We have no Marvels because we need no marvels. We live in the sea as part of the sea. To justify your excesses and your destruction, you have in the past demonized us, made us symbols of evil. Now, for the most part, you simply mythologize us. But we are living, breathing, thinking...need I go on? You have gone on producing your Marvels—and missing the marvels all about you in every moment.

I love the horizon, despite the Killing Fleet that loomed there in my youth. During my roving, I often spyhop, looking out at this juncture of worlds, sometimes serrated, sometimes a fine line, and sometimes a nebulous merging of sea and sky. I like that this boundary between my domain and the domain of the birds can be at once exact (this is *air*, and this is *water*) and unclear—always the same and always changing. And I admire the birds, their flight, their soaring and swooping. Their swimming through air.

When, as now, I spy an albatross, I know I am arriving in warmer waters. I am venturing far enough south that I will find companionship soon enough. A solitary albatross is for me, paradoxically, a harbinger of clan and kinship. And yet, like me, the albatross is always wandering. Large for a bird, with a wingspan of ten feet or more. Tenacious, able to cross vast stretches, thousands of miles, of open sea. Never rushing and never resting. And never returning home except to breed.

I suppose I see myself in the albatross, too. A kinship based on neither clan nor genetics. Always roaming. Always searching. Always looking off toward the horizon. Sometimes, I don't know how, I seem to see beyond the horizon. Can the albatross? I don't really know. But perhaps you could, if you let yourself.

꧂

Your din has become more than an annoyance. Even out here in, as you would say, *the middle of nowhere.* Our world, you must remember, is essentially acoustic, and you have made the sea increasingly noisy in my lifetime. Your tankers become ever bigger, faster, more numerous—and louder. Sometimes when they roar by, I cannot think.

Our lives are anchored in our listening; it is what we do. Our societies are formed on communication, on our need to sing and to hear one another clearly. Unnatural low frequency sounds, the sort you make, disrupt our culture. You bombard us with seismic pulses. Sonar is worse, cleaving families and clans. No one, male or female, feels much like mating amid your incessant cacophony. It affects our diving and, therefore, our eating; it sometimes causes stranding.

We avoid your clamor when possible. But it is becoming less possible. I can venture farther away, but it isn't so simple for families, much less clans like the one I will soon visit. An extended family of hundreds of females and offspring can't simply leave fertile foraging grounds. They have to put up with your noise, and damage to their hearing is inevitable. But it isn't just our hearing; noise tears the very fabric of our lives.

Does this sound at all familiar?

꧂

I admit (in fact, I should have already) that I spend a lot of my time alone because of females. Or, to be more candid, because of the way we males are when we are around them. To put it bluntly, they outperform us. When we are together, they are more successful at foraging—about twice as successful. Part of that may, of course, be that when males and females are together, males don't always focus on food. Females pay better attention to us, to each other, to our young—*and* find more food.

But that's not even all of it. The older and larger I've become, the more I realize that females' outperformance of us is relative *and* absolute. And my mind certainly is not on mating the way it once was. My clicks these days are no longer the slow rhythmic sounds that herald a male's needs. No, my clicking is faster; my needs now are at once more catholic and more urgent.

Females are simply better in some ways than we males are. We grow bigger—in fact, we are the most sexually dimorphic of mammals—but our size doesn't make us better. Bigger, you see, isn't necessarily better.

☿

I do not really want to bring up mass strandings, but I must. It is something we do. My reluctance isn't based on squeamishness or on the fact that my brother died in a mass stranding. I was not, thankfully, around when he stranded with eleven of his friends on the coast of New Zealand. I was only thirteen at the time, six years younger than he, and I probably would have done something rash.

The manner of death is slow, painful, and humiliating. You lie there wholly out of your element on that gritty shore. You gasp. Your chest heaves as gravity crushes you. You slowly overheat, your own weight making you hemorrhage. You slap your flukes, causing the earth itself to shudder, but you can do nothing to move yourself back into water. You blink and roll your eyes as you suffocate. But that is not the worst of it. No, the real horror is what drove you onto that alien shore in the first place.

♎

We strand out of altruism. It makes no sense, but there it is. Yes, weather and ocean conditions, exacerbated by your noise and pollution, contribute to any initial stranding, but the truth that's so hard for me is that mass strandings are essentially *social*. When one of us strands, others follow—out of a necessity that's hard to understand, much less explain. My brother was not the first ashore that day in New Zealand.

I have only been present once for a stranding. I was forty-nine, returning to the Gulf of Alaska from a visit to my clan in the lower latitudes. My foraging for cephalopods led me in toward the coast of the continent. A truly violent storm, one that reminded me of the day my mother died, had just blown ashore. Clouds roiled, and lightning clawed the water.

I heard the alarm clicking across a great distance. The coda was not my clan's, but I still ventured shoreward, unsure of what was happening. Or, rather, sure of what was occurring but unsure of what I was doing. When I arrived at the long tapering cove, the storm had vanished over the cliffs above the beach. Its only vestiges were the eight young males glistening darkly in the sun. Light spilled across the rolling surf, their gray-brown bodies, and the pale jutting rocks. You were already infesting the area, your machines whining.

I stayed offshore, but I was, I admit, disoriented. None of the stranded eight was my kin; their dialect was unfamiliar. All were less than half my age. Though I was mature, level-headed, seemingly detached, something still pulled me toward shore. Something inside me still called me to follow. I could not save a single one of them, nor could I leave that cove until the last one expired two days later. I swam uselessly back and forth beneath the thwacking of the whirlybirds. Sirens intermittently pierced the air; machines ground louder than the waves. I forgot to eat, forgot, in fact, everything except the stranded young males' impotence and my mother's vulnerability and my aunts' perplexity when they went to her but could do nothing to untangle the cable strangling her.

Part of my consternation came from our inherent need to follow, but part went far deeper. That social cohesion that, as I have said, I still miss after decades of solitary roving bids us all to convene, even in death. Just as we did with the Killing Fleet. We are, as a species, in life together. Our willingness, our *need*, to help each other overrides everything else. The *curse* is stranding, but the *blessing* of belonging, genetically *and* culturally, outweighs it. It's part, the essential part, of being alive.

♋

When I'm close, I can hear the clan's clicking. It's early in the day, and the females and their young are spread out over dozens of miles foraging. As I approach, I clang my arrival every five seconds or so. The first to see me are a mother, her two-year-old, and an older aunt. Though they don't know me—only the aunt has ever met me—they are unabashed in their greeting. All three rub me as we dance along, my old skin sloughing. I roll gently, basking in their movements, my role to graciously receive their ministrations. My clangs quiet to clicks.

I've already heard two other large males in the area, but they are bent on breeding—and I am not. Their clicks are slower and deeper than mine. I will tolerate their presence; they will be less tolerant of each other, a loose alliance that will soon break. The females' relationships are far more complex, an interwoven pattern of personal preferences that are most often lost on us males.

Soon, the matriarch appears. She and I mated long ago, and our son has been out roving for more than twenty years. She looks older now, her dorsal calluses thicker and her flukes more worn. Her codas, though, are tender as her jaw grazes affectionately along mine.

In the afternoon, the clan congregates. Or, rather, *we* convene, thirty-four of us, for I remain the center of attention. The newborns especially are drawn to me, my size making them giddy as they slide along my belly and back. Few of the young have met me before, and many have never even heard of me, but they gather around me as though I am some peripatetic grandfather home at last to spin his seafaring tales. And, I suppose, that's exactly what I am.

The energy pulsing through the water intoxicates me, and before I know it I'm loosing a splendid series of lobtails, Cross-Overs that shake the sky. I am, for a moment, young again, touched by others and untouched by Killing Fleets and tangled cable and lethal Marvels and Black Death and monumental garbage and mass strandings. My joy is contagious. The young breach with ecstasy, crash-splashing until the water froths. Their mothers lobtail their ovations, and even the old aunts and the matriarch side-fluke together, turning and turning in our ancient dance. And I...I spyhop to take it all in.

♊

I have been alone so much for so long that I have all but forgotten...No, that's not true. I have never forgotten that when

I was young I was touched each day, each hour. My mother's touch mattered to me as much as her milk. Her nudges and strokes, her nuzzling and rubbing, meant the world to me. Whenever she returned from a deep dive, I swam her belly before feeding. She ran her head from my jaw to my flukes. My skin, already wrinkled even then, tingled every time. When my mother died, my aunts took over. It was not the same, but it was still good, still necessary. And my rolling and sliding with my cousins cleaned us—and often provided the best moments of my day. All manner of touch matters. Perhaps not as overtly as hearing or seeing, but in its own way just as importantly. And it's good to be back now, even for a few moments, among those who touch me.

♄

The clan is good, all in all, though we've never quite recovered from the Killing Fleet massacres. Our numbers are not what they once were, and our birthrate is down. Not yet inexorably, but dangerously. We remain close to the edge of that deep trench into eternal darkness. The threats now are more subtle, but every bit as real—and far more pervasive. The sudden swooping of the Killing Fleet has been supplanted by the gradual menace that I feel in this current.

As we approach the winter solstice, the water here in the Pacific near the Galapagos is tepid—warmer than when I was young. The increase isn't yet great, just two or three degrees, but it may make all the difference in the world. Warm water is pooling here, and the earth's cycle is being altered. Warm water buries cool water. Cold, salty water sinks, taking nutrients with it. The thermocline, which used to be about 140 feet here, is now about 500 feet. Most of the fish and small squid are gone. The clan has to range farther and dive deeper for food. But this isn't about us. Not really.

It's less windy now, except during storms, which grow more fierce. The air is both warmer and wetter. Ten of the last fifteen years have been the hottest I've known. Storms are more frequent as well as more intense. Is this a fluctuation in my lifetime, or something permanent? Is it merely a difference of degree, or a difference of kind? When does a difference of degree *cause* a difference of kind? I don't know, but I do know that something is happening here. Something that's trying to teach us how small our world really is...how interrelated all of our weather is—from my summer grounds in the Arctic to these equatorial waters in winter...how bound we all are in this moment....

Could I be wrong about this? No. These climate changes are not merely the flow in the ebb of one individual's life. They are occurring. My clan *lives* amid them. The only question is, How drastic will the consequences be?

♋

The sudden silence tells me something is wrong. At the edge

of the clan's range, I am at depth, foraging in total darkness, when the clicking above me stops. Orcas. Our only predators other than you.

Killer whales is a misnomer—Orcas are killers, but they are no whales. They are *blackfish*, closer to dolphins but incorrectly perceived as one of us because of their size. Though I don't, you would think them huge—typically, twenty-four feet and nine tons. They don't really look like me either. Black and white always, with white patches behind their dark eyes. A rounded head that tapers to a point, and a prominent, even pointy, dorsal fin.

Though they are our natural enemies, I must admit, grudgingly, that they are fast and smart. Their top speed, thirty knots, is one-and-a-half times mine. Their brains are larger, relatively, than ours, though not absolutely. They remain in close-knit families their whole lives, each clan singing in its own dialect. And, they always work together, especially in their ferocious attacks. If they did not murder our young, I would tolerate, even respect them.

I stop clicking and start rising, the continued quiet telling me that the attack hasn't yet begun. I break the thermocline, pass into warm water. By the time I reach light, mad clicking showers me. The sorties have begun. The family under attack, three adult females, two immature males, and a baby, has taken to the surface, a smart move. There is no refuge in the open sea, and no hope of running. The surface takes a dimension from the enemy (at least, an *aquatic* enemy)—an attack can't come from above. And, you can catch a breath without breaking ranks. Unfortunately, the family has taken a flukes-out defensive position. When we're attacked, we form tight circles, our young in the center, our heads or our flukes facing the enemy. There are advantages to each—we gnash *and* we flail—but I favor heads-out so you can see exactly what's attacking you. Eight Orcas, including two large males, are flashing at the family's formation, trying to breach it. Blood is already in the water.

♂

Rage. My power still surges in moments of ire. Water flees, and air shivers. The Orcas strike repeatedly at the smaller mother, driving her from the defensive circle. They are not after her—they know her baby will panic, and the formation will disintegrate. White light exploding in my brain, I hurl myself at the three Orcas slicing her from her family.

Two of the Orcas fly at me. One arcs at my back and bites hard just aft of my head crease. He shakes his head to tear me, but my tough skin and thick blubber slow him for a second—a lethal second. They want blood in the water, they will have blood in the water. All in, all the way, I roll and rip my flukes, crushing his pointed snout and mouth still agape with a chunk of my flesh. Turning his brain to a sponge. I spin as the second Orca, a larger male with a wavy dorsal fin, slashes me across the head, his teeth raking me from blowhole to upper jaw. I jerk my head, my jaws clamping him just fore of his flukes. If I had upper teeth, I'd cut clear through. I soar in a world of silver light. Blood pounds in my head, swirls around me in the water.

Still clenching, I breach and whip the Orca, all nine tons of him, against the surface. Stunned, he starts to roll. I am at his neck, clutching fast, ripping out his throat. Blowing. Sucking air. Submerging. Torpedoing at the third Orca the wounded mother is fighting. Seizing its whole head. Mauling. Mangling. Light flaming all about me.

The final five Orcas run from my fury. As I escort the mother back to her family, I am exhausted. Utterly spent. The world fades to blue again—blue and red. The blood running from my snout is warm. The salt water sears my injured back. The mother is slashed below her right flipper; tentacles of torn intestine trail her. I will live, but she will not.

The large Orca with the wavy fin sinks slowly, his white belly up and his bright blood pluming. The first Orca slips sideways, the hunk of my back still in his mashed mouth. The third's pool of blood spreads, a signal for scavengers. Mother and baby nuzzle and nudge. The family rolls around me, clicking approbation. But I only swim away. I must be alone— alone with the savage truth I have always known about myself. I am the *killer whale*.

♉

When I've put some distance between the family and myself, I surface. Spyhopping, I see nothing but sea and sky and high sparse drifting white clouds. The swell is gentle, the wind light. Blood still seeps from my head and back, but the physical wounds aren't my concern. My blood may well attract sharks, but even they are not stupid enough to attack me in this moment. My anger slowly evaporates in the vastness of the open ocean.

I'm not sorry. Not at all. I was provoked, and I responded. But I am frightened by my fury. I don't otherwise harbor fears. The world exists. Death occurs to each of us no matter what currents we have swum. And pain is pain. It occurs, too. It is part of life, part of the great current. I am, as I have said, a gentle soul. I love touch, but I'm too shy, too solitary, to stick around for the family's adulation. I was not heroic—I was incensed, and the white light of rage flowed through me.

Can the world itself experience that infuriating flash of light? You wouldn't think so, but the world's time is far deeper than our time. The Earth breathes just as we do—but only once each year, a single inhalation and exhalation. We find it difficult to fathom this breadth and depth of time, the world's slow cycle of life. But what is happening here in the Eastern Pacific and there at the North Pole—the melting and the calving, the pooling and the storms—is a mere instant in the world's life. At what point does the destruction and pollution, the emissions and toxic wastes—the flotsam and jetsam that you insist on flinging ever overboard—provoke the planet? Is this *the* moment, the blind blink of deep time?

☿

In the aftermath of the Orca attack, I swim westward, farther into the ocean's expanse, away from the clan to which I belong. The horizon retreats in every direction. I need this time alone. I know all too well that we exist in time, but often it flows unevenly. It fluctuates. Now, for instance, time is an eel. It slithers and twists, turns, stops, waits, strikes. I keep on my way until I can find again the pulse of this planet, the regular beat of the world, and finally rid myself of this eel that stalks me.

The life of the world is *not* eternal. It is so vast that it seems eternal, but it is not. Each of us is alive, a part of this living planet, for only a short time. But the eternal does exist—and you can discover it during your brief time. It is here and now. It exists for me in the suspended moment, in the balance between rising and falling as I breach. In the moment when Architeuthis and I strike at once. The moment in which the newborn, nudged to the surface, breaks into sky and takes his first breath. The moment in which, while I am spyhopping, the sea stops and the light unfurls.

☿

Despite the tone of my voice, the movements of this song,

and the refrains to which I return, I do not hate you. As you have heard, I'm perfectly capable of fury, but I am not sunk in animosity. I cannot sustain malevolence. I understand that you have become so enamored of your Marvels that you are blind to their consequences, so bewitched by your creations that you ignore the concomitant destruction. But it is time, your moment in time, your moment beyond time. You must discover the world anew and let it take your breath afresh— and you must fall in love with it, all in, all the way.

Just as I find it hard to hate, I find it difficult to love. I loved my mother, was devoted to her, would have defended her, tooth and fluke, until the end. I never knew my father well enough to love him. The idea of him, yes, but not *him*. My siblings? Cousins and friends? Yes, I've felt loyalty and caring. I would have, in certain situations, given my life for them. The females with whom I mated? In those times, perhaps. And later, when they were the caretakers of my offspring. My children? Well, yes, them, too. But I never lived with them, never was the parent each of their mothers was. And I always moved on, driven both by our norms and by something inside me.

But I am able to love this world—and life itself. A deep and abiding love. And that, *sometimes*, is enough. Not always. But sometimes. You are built for love, as I am. As are we all. This I know: I love the sea and the air, the seasons, the journey that is my life, the life of each and every one of us, each day and every night. I love each blow from my spout when I rise from a long, dark dive. Each and every light-blasted breath.

And this is why, against all odds, I offer you this song. So you, too, may love every moment of every day. Each breath. Each moment in and out of time. The spreading light and the gathering darkness. Warm air and cold rain. Every morsel of food. The presence of others. Voices singing. The touch of this being and that. Even pain, great and small. All of it.

♉

Pressure mounts. The water is warm, above 80 degrees, and the air thick. Clouds tower, but there is no front. Heat and vapor rise. Thunderstorms converge, and wind soars. The bands of clouds are already radiating. Something violent this way comes, and the gathering storm will tear the stillness, tear every thought we have.

This terrible beauty beginning to whirl around me makes me think about the mystery at the core of each of our lives. The mystery from which all things—sea salt and sharks' teeth and ice songs and storm centers—emanate. Life is, in essence, aqua incognita. But this mystery is just that; it cannot *save* the world now. The current changes suggest that you have placed your Marvels above our mystery. Or worse, that you have set yourselves up as Destroyers, bringing devastation down on all of us. You need humility—before the sacredness of being, the interwoven fabric of life in the sea and sky and on land. You must again remember, come once more to understand, that you are part of the fabric of life, not separate from it—and certainly not above it.

☊

The storm is immensely powerful, the most potent event on the planet. Your most destructive Marvels are minute by comparison. The seas grow so rough that even the most titanic of your tankers flee the region. The wind and the electrical noise drown every sound you make. The swells rise to forty and then fifty feet, the periods between them brief and erratic. Spindrift screams, and clouds streak at over 120 knots. On the surface, what is air and what is water becomes moot. I must breach, as full out as when I was young, to catch my breath.

I go deep to avoid the chaos in the world above. The power of this sea, the energy in this storm, is enough to make me fathom unknown waters, and enough, in and of itself, to make me understand nothing. Nothing but the existence of the world. Nothing but this storm. The universe shrinks to this black hole of energy, this storm, here and now. The Earth in this moment becomes the mystery unadorned.

☊

I breach in the eye of the storm. The eye is small, perhaps twelve miles across. Clouds in the eyewall rip by at 150 knots, but here the wind is only a tenth that speed. Albatrosses, trapped by the wall's dark clouds rising to fantastic heights, will go wherever the storm takes them. The storm itself is traveling toward higher latitudes at about ten knots, and I can keep up for a time, swimming here in the relative tranquility of the eye. The seas remain rough and confused, but I am not. All about me, energy whirls—perhaps a million cubic miles of atmosphere is enclosed by the storm—and I exist for a moment in the still point at its center. Energy flows through me from the wounds in my head to the torn tips of my flukes.

It doesn't matter what you call that which binds us, each to the other and all to the sea and sky and land. In this relative stillness, I can feel the flow of the world. And when I am roving, I can as well. Not merely in the swells or the current or the thermocline. It is something else, something more, something that permeates the world but isn't evident unless you yield to it. Wherever you are, whatever you're doing. I've thought about all of this, and I understand that I can't know it in the way I know currents and depths and the pull of the poles. I also realize I must sound like some quixotic rhapsodist breaching beneath a full moon. But this energy abides. I—we all—breathe it each moment. And it is, ultimately, why I harbor no bitterness.

♉

The vast power of this storm reminds us all that our world is, indeed, small. The storm will affect weather across the planet.

It will touch every one of us in some way. It is not merely the albatrosses that will be displaced. We will all, in ways large and small, be disheveled. This is no mere cod flapping its tail: currents will be altered and winds disturbed. Food resources will decline, destroyed or redistributed so that many will starve and a few will grow fat. It's the way the world works.

Though the storm cuts a wide swath, I swim against its prevailing path, breaching intermittently for breath, and thus in three days free myself of it (if not its consequences). The Orca's slashes across my head are scarring, but my dorsal wound festers. Perhaps, ironically, I am being eaten by bacteria.

I'm also, though I'd rather not admit it, a little worn down by the Orca attack and the storm. Don't misunderstand me. I'm not at all tired of this song. But I need to find seas less vexed and winds more tempered. I am feeling, well, a little old—and yet I am in no way ready to feed the sharks. I still must seek a newer world. I must continue to strive and search and sing. As must we all.

♉

The vestiges I find in the storm's wake disturb me. Remnants not just of its power but also of your pollution. Dead albatrosses and gannets are scattered about, of course. There is always carrion for scavengers after a potent storm. But I also encounter small floating islands of debris—not just torn branches and tangled vines, but your synthetic refuse blown into the open ocean by this storm. Your detritus is indigestible, but that doesn't stop marine life, even Cetaceans, from ingesting it. We eat what we find, even when it's inedible.

What I can't see is even worse than what I can. Chemicals and other artificial particles I can barely discern taint the water. Storms invariably stir the toxins you have discharged into the sea, and plastics, it turns out, are pelagic, too. Perhaps 50,000 adulterated motes float in every square mile of ocean. And, rather than decompose, they disintegrate into smaller, but no less noxious, specks.

You have, I understand, used the sea as a garbage dump for a thousand generations. But in my lifetime, the life of one being, the problem has become exponentially worse—so much so that this storm's detritus is a mere stain compared to the debris already heaped and swirling within the North Pacific Gyre. The mass of plastic floating there is five or six times that of the zooplankton. In fact, the trash cycling within the gyre is so thick that no Cetacean, Baleen or Toothed, would traverse the area anymore. And it was, you must remember, not really so long ago that my friends and I wandered there unbound and unbounded. Now it is an unnatural archipelago well on its way to forming a septic continent mid-ocean.

Or worse, the garbage patch is becoming the malevolent eye of a far slower but far deadlier cyclonic event, a storm of sewage you build each day of every year. The ocean is one entity, one organ—and when you contaminate one part of it you inevitably foul all of it. You are currently disgorging your waste so fast that none of us can fully comprehend its impact on life. Not just marine life, but *all* life.

♉

These dark thoughts drive me north and west, farther from my clan, farther from decomposing Orcas, and farther from the storm's wake. In fact, beyond Bikini and Enewetak, those infamous islands of my youth. I could keep going. Tempt fate. Venture closer to the islands where your Killing Fleets still loom and the Death Factories still operate. I could *attack* their Killers—I am capable of it—but it's a futile gesture. A suicidal mission.

I have always understood, of course, that you are the ones who operated the Death Factory, disemboweling and tearing apart my kin. You detonated the heinous Marvel and loosed the Black Death and laid the strangling cable. You persist in defiling the sea with your excrement. I am the Killer Whale, and you are the Destroyers. We must understand that about each other.

And, we need to go on. It's time. You have become the Destroyers, but you remain the world's best and only hope. I cling to this belief as I once clung to my mother's nipple. We are the only ones able to sing this song, and you are the only ones capable of undoing the damage you have done. I know

that the very egocentrism that drives so much of your luna-
cy may now compel you to rescue our world. Here, after all,
is our final paradox: in the face of the current climatic cataclysm, self-interest and altruism become one. The only way
to save yourself is to save us all. We, as I have been chanting
all along, are, and have always been, inexorably entwined—
bound fast to each other and to this world. Now is the time to
take action, to take your place as we wheel through our lives
and the life of this planet. This is your brief moment. Seize it.

♉

No, I will not venture toward the Islands of the Killing Fleets.
I understand that it is better to live humbly, to go on singing my song, than to die dramatically far from my clan. I am
pelagic, even peripatetic, but my song belongs to all of us. I
may look like an island unto myself, but I am not. No being
is. We all need to be social to survive.

It is my role, given my age, my gender, and my size, to
wander alone, to recall moments in my life, and to sing for
you. My song matters to our survival, but the song is mean-
ingless if it were not for others, us and you. We are all in this
together as living creatures, as mammals, as social beings
who share a home.

I breach under a gibbous moon. The vastness of the night
sky makes me feel small. And the sheer number of wheeling
stars mid-ocean takes my breath. The Milky Way spreads

light like phosphorescent krill across the sky. A shooting star flares—an ephemeral traveler, as we all are.

I lobtail, a fine Dorsal Down that cracks the heavens. I become drunk for a moment on air and memory. I will, I know now, return to my clan, at least for a time. I smack a dozen Cross-Overs. Though the festering wound on my back breaks open, I am as giddy as a two-year-old.

I suck air as though it *is* life. It is life, you know. We *are* air and water. Sometimes I am acutely aware of it in every cell— as though I were just born. The night air is bright, inside me and out—and the dark sky shimmers. Energy swirls around me, cycling through me and this world. Water flows in unfathomable currents. The air clicks and claps.

Through it, you will find meaning. Through it, you will understand what must be done. You will comprehend that the solutions to our current global problems lie not in more and larger Marvels but in balance, in letting yourself be touched by the world, in surrendering to your moment in time, in living deeply each day, in taking action that affirms life. Locally, wherever you are, and globally.

JAY AMBERG is the author of
ten books. He has taught high school
and college students since 1972.